The Freedom... Cage

TO Eli and Jaffa

my best friends and some time like
a mother and father to me and fought
like one and especially Elis and I yelled
at each other. But I love them

LUONG UNG-LAI

ISBN: 1475273541

ISBN 13: 9781475273540

Library of Congress Control Number: 2012907745
CreateSpace, North Charleston, SC

For my Ma and Grandfather

To have a ma and grandpa like
You
Is like looking at the
Sun
Shining through the
Cloud,
And its brighten the
Earth,

And its shines into my
Eyes

The sweetness of
The summer's wind,
Keeps blowing toward my
Nose

Just want to let
You
Know, that your
Names
Will always be
Known,

Keem Lai and Wong Lai

Yours Moy
(Written in 2005)

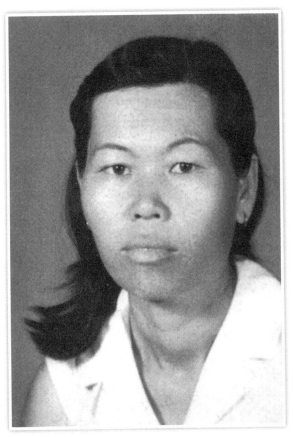

Keem is Sue Chae-(Star) Lai's nickname. 1935 to 1977

Ma was forty-one when she had this picture taken in Phnom Penh for her last passport. Ma passed away and went to heaven at the age of forty-two. Her nickname, Keem, means pipa. Pipa is an instrument used to play music since the old age in China till present day.

Wong Lai, 1913 or 1925 to 1977

I don't know how old Grandpa was or where this picture was taken.
This is the only picture I have of him by himself.

A New Reversion of

The Freedom... Cage

(With new editing 2012)

The dialogue in this story was originally in Chinese and Khmer. I tried, to the best of my ability, to translate the Chinese and Khmer/Cambodian verbal languages into English. Some words in Chinese and Khmer don't exist in English, and some English words don't have correlates in Chinese and Khmer.

You may find that the dialogue in this book sounds strange. I have tried to translate the Chinese and Khmer directly into English, keeping some of the features of those languages. For example, in Chinese and in Khmer (*I may be wrong in Khmer*), there are no verb tenses; instead of "I went" and "I will go," one says, "I go yesterday" and "I go tomorrow," respectively. There are also no articles and no plural markers, so for "two men," the Khmer say "man, man," or for "the two girls," in English, "girl, girl" or "girl two the." The word order of much of the Cambodian language is the opposite of that in English. However, Chinese differs from Cambodian; we say "one woman" or "two woman" or "one group woman," meaning many women; we also say "the moon bright, bright," meaning the moon is very bright and "open your eye big, big," meaning open your eyes bigger, in English.

Please keep in mind that this book is *based on memories*. Some parts may not be as detailed as you would like or may not give you a clear picture of what happened. This book may shock you. But the world is evil. May we all learn from our past mistakes and make this world a better place to live in. May there be peace on earth.

Preface

Before

The Freedom...Cage

This book is a true account of my experiences and memories. It took all my willpower to write this book. All the nightmares and heartaches I had tried to forget came back to me as I wrote it. Although it is my story, I had to refer to myself in the third person by my childhood nickname Moy, which means "little sister." That was the name my family used to address me. This child I was lived through all the horrors described in this book, and she is still a part of me. I can't forget her or what she went through, or I'll die. She has made me strong enough to fight off the horror of my memories. If I had used the first person in telling her story, it would have been like going back and reliving it all again. And I'm not strong enough to do that.

My grandparents and parents came from China, but I was born in Cambodia. My ma gave birth to me on the first morning the lions ruled the streets and wakened the sleeping dragons, when the sun was barely risen. Almost every street was filled with the sounds of the drums, fifes, oboes, and cymbals playing "The Eight Angels" music from tape players. (There are seven males and a female angel on a quest cross the ocean.) People knelt on both knees and lit small red candles on both sides of their loved ones' spirit stands (small cans of uncooked rice wrapped in red paper) and the Earth Uncle's (sort of like the local town's or city's spirit) as well. While the white dragons zigzagged upward toward heaven at the tips of the burning incense in people's hands, people prayed and asked their loved ones' spirits and the Earth Uncle to chase the bad people away and bring them good health and good fortunes for the New Year.

Children screamed in excitement and ran, following the sound of the drums and cymbals. They watched with big, happy smiles on their faces. The performers jumped, turned, and hopped around doing the lions' dances inside the red, yellow, white, gold, blue, and silver lion costumes. Children covered their ears. The loud sound of firecrackers exploding at people's front doors chased away the bad spirits and brought in good luck. They were welcoming the mighty *dragon* into the *New Year*; it was February 13, 1964.

I was born in a small house in Siem Reap, in the city of Angkor, on the east side of Cambodia. The house my mother gave birth to me in was smaller than my bedroom is now. Ma and I shared a double bed. It was pushed against the front wall. The door was next to our bed. A tall dresser was pushed up against the opposite wall. At night, Grandpa had his folding bed between our bed and the dresser in front of a tiny little window.

There was a small hallway from the front door to the back door. We didn't have chairs or a table. We sat on the gray cement floor and had our meals. The pots and pans sat nearby on the floor next to the tall dresser. One wall of our house was the landlord's wooden wall. The rest of the walls were made of bamboo trees cut in half and bound together with ropes. The roof was covered in dry brown grasses. The water well was behind and next to the back of our little house and was shared by the whole neighborhood.

In Cambodia, about 95 percent of the businesses were outdoors, in the open public markets. The other 5 percent were indoor businesses, like the jewelry stories, some pork noodle soup shops, and so on.

While we lived in that little house, we had a five-and-dime business in the open market. We owned a small space and paid tax every day! By our business standards, the general public considered us the middle class. However, our little house's appearance was lower class. *One outhouse* was shared by the whole neighborhood. Luckily for me, I never had to use that famous neighborhood outhouse. I was simply too young and too little to make the visit.

I narrowly escaped from having to visit the famous outhouse, when we moved to our new enormous cement house (called a town house). Half of the house was used as a stockroom. Both walls were stocked up with sugar, eggs, candy, and so on. A large round table and chairs were placed against a wall in our large bedroom. Grandpa's folding bed was against a wall in the big stockroom. Grandpa owned a large motorcycle. The third part of our house was the giant, roofless common kitchen and bathroom. There was a large roof over the two cooking stoves. In the kitchen area, there was a hand-pumped well, and the bathroom was under the open sky. There was a big roof over the cement toilet; after it was used, it was flushed with a bucket of water. And the last part of our house, Ma rented to a Cambodian family.

During that period, Prince Sihanouk was the ruler of Cambodia. I remember that stores were open twenty-four hours a day. When I was a little older, Lon Nol, Sihanouk's right-hand man, took over. I learned from my grandpa that this had happened during Sihanouk's visit to China. Lon Nol was a dictator rather than a king. During his rule, stores were open from 7:00 a.m. to 9:00 p.m., and no one was allowed on the streets after 9:00 p.m. If anyone disobeyed, he or she was arrested, jailed, and fined without a trial.

I don't remember how old I was when Grandpa brought me a three-wheel bike from the capital Phnom Penh. My nanny had lunch or dinner and chased after me while I was on my bike. The general public considered my family rich. We were happy living in that big new house. Then one evening, while we were having dinner, all hell broke loose. Our large folding doors were broken down, and the policemen charged in; they were looking for my third uncle and destroyed our house. The policemen told Grandpa and Ma that Uncle had tried to become a Cambodian citizen. That was against Cambodia's law. Uncle was the first generation to be born in Cambodia. He had to be the third generation to be accepted as a Cambodian citizen. Uncle and his family didn't live with us. The policemen came looking for him in our house anyway.

Grandpa and Ma didn't want Uncle to go to jail. Money was paid under the table. The policemen sucked away all our money; every day, different policemen came looking for Uncle. In the end, Grandpa and Ma hardly had any money left. The policemen threatened to throw them in jail. Grandpa and Ma took me and fled during the night to Phnom Penh with only the clothes on our backs.

I was too young at the time to understand what was happening then. Now that I look back, I can see it was a setup by my third uncle. He wanted our house, Grandpa's large motorcycle, and our business. He shared the money he took from us with the policemen. After we fled from our new home, my third uncle and his family lived happily in our house! And the policemen were his best friends! But Grandpa and Ma were wanted by the law in Siem Reap, because they had no more money to give them. Years later, Grandpa and Ma understood what had really happened, but they still loved my third uncle. And they kept the truth from me.

In Phnom Penh, we lived in Grandpa's friend's house—in one room. Grandpa's friend had a bed; Ma and I shared a bed; and Grandpa used a folding bed. There was hardly any room to move around at night. There was a small kitchen and a small bathroom. In Phnom Penh, we made sweet fry rice cakes and sold them on the sidewalk for a living. We lived there for two years more or less, and then we went to Pailin. Now, I present to you, the story of *The Freedom... Cage*.

LUONG H UNG LAI

Ma told me this picture was taken when I was five months old. I couldn't sit up yet. And my father is hiding behind the chair, pulling my dress back, helping me sit up straight.

Prologue

Moy

I was nine years old, and it was Chinese New Year when this picture was taken in Phnom Penh.

"Where is she?"

"I don't know!"

"Don't lose. Find her!"

"There she is. Get her!"

The men are speaking in English. Heavy footsteps follow the little girl, and she runs as fast as her short legs can carry her. She runs and runs, stopping only when she gets to the big tree. Hiding behind it, she tries to catch her breath, covering her mouth with her hands so the soldiers can't hear her heavy breathing. Her small back is pressed against the big tree, and her young eyes are filled with horror—no tears...nothing but helplessness and fear that she might never escape from the deadly game of these hunters. Her hands still covering her small mouth, she moves her head cautiously to see if the soldiers are far enough away that she can make another run for her life. Seeing no movement, she starts running again. After only a few yards, her black sarong catches on the branch of a small tree, and she falls hard, face-first on the ground. Sitting up quickly, she tries to free herself with shaking hands. Blood is running down her small arms. Her black, long-sleeved shirt is torn, and her thin legs are bared by the snagged sarong. Hearing heavy footsteps close behind her, the little girl pulls desperately. Freeing the sarong, she scrambles to her feet and, without looking back, starts to run again. Her bare feet hurt. Her heart pounds in her chest. But all she cares about is saving her young life.

"Look!"

"Where?"

"There!" All five Khmer Rouge stop, and one of them bends down to pick up a scrap of black cloth from the branch. "She comes this way!" he shouts. "Let's get her!"

The men run after the thirteen-year-old girl. They wear long black cotton pants and long-sleeved shirts and carry guns. Their faces are cold and hard. If they find the girl, they will kill her without a second thought.

The girl comes to a village with small houses clustered together. Stumbling from exhaustion, she prays silently that the sun will not be born soon. In this dark, moonless night, she has a better chance to escape from her killers' hands. Somehow, she finds herself underneath one of the houses, her nose pressed to the ground. Confused, she looks up to find the silver sun is high above her head. Then, hearing voices, she sees the soldiers and a young man.

"Get over here if you want live another second!" The soldier laughs. Then he hits the young man on the side of his head with the back of his gun. "Dig your own grave if you want one. Now dig!"

The soldiers all laugh, and the young man does as he is told. When the hole is twelve or thirteen inches deep, the soldiers order the young man down on his knees. One soldier grabs his arms, pulling them far back. A second soldier raises a long knife and cuts the young man's head off. The head flies into the hole. The young man's body shakes so hard. It seems like it wants to escape its killers' hands and live again. But blood spurts out of his body in large, separate drops and then slows to a lazy shower. The Khmer Rouge laugh, as if they have won the greatest game in the world. Two of the soldiers begin pulling the clothes off the body. "You don't need these clothes now. They are for the living...and one day, their clothes will go to someone else, too." The soldiers all laugh again.

One of the Khmer Rouge turns to look at a young woman. Her face is white as paper, her body paralyzed with fear. Then she walks to the hole and stands lifeless for a moment. Suddenly, she screams in terror as the soldier starts to pull her shirt and sarong off of her. The louder she screams, the louder the soldiers laugh. Her screams and their laughter are ringing in the ears of the horrified little girl hiding under the house. Her eyes grow wider and wider. Her body shakes helplessly, as the screams and laughter seem to grow louder and louder.

Buddha help me! the child thinks. *Please help me! I can't take this anymore. Help me just to get away from these sounds.*

But the sounds don't go away. It is no longer daytime. It's dark, and I turn my head slowly, surveying my surroundings. I see my old gray winter coat hanging on the door near the bed, inside a small little rented bedroom in a house. Closing my eyes, I take a deep breath. *It was a nightmare! It isn't real!* The screaming sound is coming from the alarm clock. Usually, I hate the sound of the alarm. But today, I welcome it. I reach over to turn it off. Then I run my hands slowly over my face, finding it dry. I'm amazed that my body isn't shaking as I get out of bed. I walk from the bedroom to the bathroom and turn on the bathroom light. I wash my face and brush my teeth. Normally, I put on my makeup first, but this morning, I feel a coldness...whether of body or of mind. I put on my undershirt, high-necked pink T-shirt, and long blue pants before applying my eyeliner and gathering my books for my classes at the university. As I comb my hair before the small oval mirror, I see a young woman with flat cheekbones; a wide, pink-lipped mouth; a small, short nose; a small brown birthmark below the left nostril; brown eyes; and dark-brown hair that looks black in the orangish light. Her

3

eyes are dry but sad from the pain that can't be hidden away. Where are the tears she should be shedding? I don't know. I only know that life must go on. I look long and hard at the woman in the mirror. Then I turn away with a sigh.

Going down the stairs, I stop in front of the big Chinese mirror in the hall by the front door. As I put on my short, dark-red jacket, again, I see the woman in the mirror, head high and shoulders square. But her eyes are very sad...and dry, too dry.

I don't believe you are as strong as you look! I know you too well. You may look strong, but inside, you are cold, weak, and shaking with fear. You may lie to others, but you can't fool me! You know why? Because I know you from inside out, I think.

As I continue to stare at the mirror, the face of the sad-eyed woman slowly fades into that of a ten-year-old girl. She sits near a well in front of the house in Pailin, in northwestern Cambodia. The child's head hangs low. A woman in long black silk pants and a navy short-sleeved shirt bends over her, scissors in hand. Her free hand holds the child's head still, as she cuts the girl's dark-brown hair. They speak in the Chau Chow, a Chinese dialect.

1
The Freedom...
Cage

"Ma, can I keep my hair long this year?" the girl asked with a frown, knowing perfectly well the answer would be "No."

"No. When you a little older, you can have long hair. Now be still, or I cut one side shorter than the other," the black-haired, black-eyed woman told her stubborn little daughter, who could get away with almost anything—except having long hair.

"How much older?" Moy demanded, pouting.

"Be nice, and pull your lower lip in or it fall off," Keem warned her daughter. "How you like to have only the top one...?"

"It's in! It's in!" the child whispered, eyebrows pulled together. Without turning and looking at Keem, she knew her mother was smiling because her threat had succeeded. *How did she know my lip was pushed out?* Moy asked herself. *She can't even see it with my head bent down like this. Ah! She's my ma and knows everything I do.*

Not everything, the child thought with a big grin on her small face. *Ma doesn't know that I eat pork noodle soup almost every day or that I see each movie at least three times. It's not my fault I go behind her back. She never wants to go anywhere. All she wants to do is make money and save money! Not like Grandpa. He makes money but still goes to see a movie or two and goes out for lunch sometimes. And he buys me toys...a sword and a three-wheeled bicycle. But not Ma...she wants to save every penny.*

Well, not every penny. She buys me toys too...lot of toys! She wants me to have everything like other kids have. Let me see now, Moy thought, her eyes narrowing. *Oh yes! She bought me eight dolls with blue eyes and yellow hair, from six inches to thirty inches tall. She bought six goldfish, one long and one short battery-operated gun. She and Grandpa both bought me a whole set of girls' toys—pots and pans and so forth. And—*

"Your nose touch ground yet?" The girl's thoughts were interrupted by Keem's question. Then she realized that her mother hadn't been doing anything to her hair for some time. Moy looked up and gave her mother a smile so big, her eyes closed. "Flat-nosed lady!" Her mother whispered, smiling indulgently at her stubborn little daughter and patting her tiny nose. The girl's smile grew even bigger, because that pat on the nose meant a lot of love. "Spoiled child!" her mother said with laughter in her voice, as her face filled with love for her only child. Keem knew she and her father had spoiled the girl. But it was hard not to spoil this lovable ten-year-old.

"Ma, you done with my hair yet?" Moy asked, toying with a handful of long hair that had been cut off. Before her mother could answer, she added sulkily, "All those people come here tomorrow?"

"Yes. And you try be nice!"

"Nice, nice, nice! Why I the one be nice? They never nice to me. They hate me!"

"I not care what you think. You my daughter, and you do as I say!"

The girl's face was now between her mother's hands, and two pairs of angry eyes stared at each other. Keem spoke with irritation in her voice. "Tomorrow is Chinese New Year, and I want you be nice to everyone."

"All they want is money, just money! You think they come here to see you and Grandpa? If you not have money for them, they not even look at you and Grandpa, much less talk to you. They all the same!" The girl's voice grew bitterer; Keem just stared at her. "It not just at New Year they come. They here almost every week...this one or that one, always after your and Grandpa's money. And that mine money too!"

"Enough!" Keem hissed. But that didn't stop her loose-tongued daughter.

"They sleep till their butt root to their bed. While the sole of my two foot nearly wear off. And all my tooth nearly fall out. From run around and beg people buy bread and Lucky Ticket!"

"Poor child! Your tooth all fall out. You not have any tooth. Poor child!" Her mother's hard face had turned soft. Her eyes were sad, but a little smile played at her lips. And she teased her loose-tongued daughter. "Let me see, Grandma, if any tooth still in your mouth?" Moy's mouth was already wide open. "One, two, three..." her mother counted with laughter in her voice but pride in her face. "Why, I see all of them still there!"

8

"They all there, but they all loose," the girl whispered and then added with a grin, "because of all candy I eat!"

Mother and daughter broke out laughing. Keem looked at her daughter with pride and then said softly, "If there a way to go, there a way to come. Remember that...you hear?"

"I hear." Moy looked up at her mother with a frown on her small face. *Now what does she mean by that?* The girl narrowed her eyes as she thought, *Why can't she just say what she means? But no, she wants to keep me guessing. And I'll go on guessing till my hair turns gray and my back humps up till it touches the sky and my head hangs down; till my long, white hair sweeps the floor. Whatever it means, I see a lot of things going, then come; that's a fact.*

"And remember. Speak nicely and make friend with them, tomorrow. It New Year Day, and you act like well-brought-up young lady, not like some silly child. And remember, be respectful to everyone, young or old, you hear?" It was a demand, not a request. Moy knew the difference. She always got a pat on the nose with a request, a pat that meant love, respect, and pride. "If you can't stand them, get out of their way. If they try push you to the edge, stand high, high— stand up straight and be strong, and don't let them trap you. Push back!" Keem whispered the last two words into Moy's ears. Then she got up and went into the house without looking back at her daughter, who still sat by the well with her knees drawn up to her chin.

Moy cocked her head to one side and stared at her mother's back, her eyes wide and confused. *What does she mean by that? Does she want me to fight back or not? Ooo! How I want to kick all of them on their butts, kick them so hard their head would touch the ceiling. And when they came down, I'd kick them again so hard. They could feel the bones in their lazy butts fall out of their pants.* Her head came up sharply at her mother's voice calling from the house.

"No argument tomorrow. Remember that too!"

Another demand without a pat on the nose, Moy thought with a smile.

* * *

Chinese New Year was the day that whole families would get together—even those who didn't like each other, let alone love one other. That was exactly how it was for the little girl in the light-pink dress that came to just above her knees. She wore a pair of nude-colored shoes with one-inch heels. Her hair was a bit above her ears now. Moy did her best to smile at everyone, even those whose eyes she'd have loved to tear from their faces. Their eyes would brighten whenever they saw money. Their lips never closed as they spoke of their greed.

"How much ning Grandpa give you in the red envelope, Moy?" Pig demanded with a serious face and voice.

Without thinking, the girl pulled out the money. No one needed to tell her that she'd get more money from her beloved grandfather than any of them. *Because Grandpa loves me best,* the girl thought. "Let's see now..." The girl paused and looked at her cousin with big, innocent eyes. "Why not you tell me how much you get...Big Brother?" She forced the last two words between her teeth.

"I get a hundred ning. That what Grandpa give *me!*" Pig's chin was high as he spoke loud enough for everyone in the room to hear.

"Really? Wow! A hundred ning? I bet Grandpa not give me a hundred ning. You be sure of that!" Moy looked all innocence, and from the corner of her eye, she saw her mother trying hard not to laugh. Keem was successful. But Moy's grandfather broke out laughing and pretended that it was brought on by his youngest granddaughter. Pig was so curious. He would have poked his head inside the red envelope if it had been big enough. Moy's small hand pushed her cousin's head away. She kept the same innocent tone as she pulled the money out. "It not that much," she said, pausing with a smile. "Only a thousand ning," she added, showing her cousin a handful of hundred-ning bills. "See, only ten." With a wide grin, she turned on her heels, leaving a red-faced Pig to stare after her.

Pig indeed! Moy thought the name suited him just fine. He looked like one, ate like one, and even slept like one. He had a round face; big, round black eyes; black hair; and small, round lips. *All he does is sleep, eat, and go to the movies. All his seven sisters and brothers are just like him. And he's four whole years older than me. If I was anything like that, Ma and Grandpa would beat the life out of me from the time I could walk!*

"You insult your big brother!" Pig's mother's angry laugh got everyone's attention and stopped Moy in her tracks, one foot in and one foot out the door. But the girl turned slowly and spoke sweetly to her aunt.

"Why, Big Aunt? Big Brother ask me question, and I answer. You think that insult him?"

"You have sharp mouth!" Pig's mother was nearly out of her chair. She pointed her finger at Moy, her round cheeks red with danger and her small black eyes darkening in rage.

"How I know how food taste if my mouth not sharp?" Moy cocked her head, a small smile playing on her lips. Pig's mother looked like she would murder her in cold blood if she could.

"She always want to win, no matter what!" Moy's fourth uncle put in from the other side of the room, before his big sister-in-law could think of anything else to say.

"That so? That why your chest still hurt. You *not* want to win fight with your friend's younger brother two year ago?" Moy's small lips tightened, and her eyes narrowed to match her uncle's fierceness.

"She the most stubborn little girl I ever see," Moy's youngest aunt exclaimed before her brother could defend himself from his young attacker.

"You never see me before? Small Aunt, you see me almost every week. Matter of fact, I your niece. You know? The daughter of your big sister...woman you ask for money?" Moy took a step closer to her youngest aunt, looked at her with wide, innocent eyes, and went for blood. "I granddaughter of your father... you know, that man right there, who just give you a red envelope?" Moy pointed to her grandpa. He sat, clad in long navy pants and a white, long-sleeved shirt, on a chair next to the big round table by the wall.

Though his lips seemed to smile, his long, handsome face was hard; his eyes were hidden behind his heavy eyeglasses. Moy didn't really want to look him in the eye right then. But he didn't act angry or pay much attention to her. And her mother was busy on the other side of the room. But Moy knew. Ma, Grandpa, and everyone in the two-room house were all ears.

"You never back down!" her third uncle began.

But Grandpa's big, deep voice silenced everyone, even the three-year-old.

"Today New Year, children."

"Yes," Moy's third uncle muttered but kept his hard eyes on her.

Then everyone returned to what they had been doing before the argument. And Moy was out the door and on her way to play with the neighbor's children.

New Year's lunch and dinner went smoothly after that. At the round table with Grandpa Wong and Keem were Moy's three uncles and four aunts. Her seventeen boy and girl cousins sat on the mat on the floor. There were chicken, duck, and pork rice; vegetables with pork or chicken; soft drinks—black, white, and orange colors—in glass bottles; candy; and many other delicacies for the New Year's feast. The older people ate, talked, and laughed, while the children screamed, yelled, and fought until their parents threatened to take their red envelopes away if they didn't behave.

But one child wasn't fighting or screaming at anyone. She was enjoying herself outside in the front yard. Her back leaning against the water well, she had a bowl of food on her lap—two big chicken legs, rice, and mushrooms with pork—and a bottle of some kind of soft drink next to her. Her legs were straight out in front of her. Her mind was on nothing but the delicious food. Occasionally, her mother or grandfather would come out, pat her head, and smile down at her. She would cock her head back and smile. Though no one knew it, this was to be the final year of hate and love for the whole family together.

* * *

Nineteen seventy-four was gone, and 1975 had begun. The girl was now eleven. One day in January, Moy saw that her mother looked terrified. Keem's eyes were filled with fear, and she seemed to be shaking. In the afternoon, Keem asked Moy to sit with her, behind their small cigarette table, in the store near the bus station. Sitting on the small, round, four-legged stool, her back against a dead tree, Keem told Moy about her fear.

"I dream last night that nearly scare me to death. I see many Black Shirt come into city and town and chase people from their home," she said, referring to the Khmer Rouge. "I see hundred and thousands of people walk and walk, not know where to go." Moy looked up as her mother's voice became shaky. She saw Keem's eyes widen as she recalled the nightmare. "All house empty, no living soul on highway, road, and street...not even dog! Then I see people cry for food and water. Their stomachs big, big, but they just skin and bones. Their eyes big, big, fill with sorrow. People use leaf for spoon, small branch for chopstick, coconut shell for bowl, tree trunk for table and chair. They dig hole in the ground to make cooking stove. Ground their bed, and sky their roof. Old or young, everyone have black sarong and long-sleeved shirt, but no shoe. Their foot bleed; they walk barefoot up mountain to work there.

"I see Black Shirt take people from their home and kill them, because they don't like them. Or because they walk out of town, when Black Shirt tell them not to. Or just kill them for fun! Dead have only blanket to cover them, and some not even have that. Somebody put into hole by their family, and other lie on ground covered only with some leaf.

"All little child sent far away from parent. All husband and wife separate. Everyone work and live in forest. Everywhere I look, I see only tree and black. Everywhere and everything black!"

Moy looked hard at the ground, unaware her mother had stopped speaking. She didn't know what to make of the nightmare. But it sounded very real and very scary. *But it is only a dream,* she thought. *I have nightmares too...people flying or killing each other...but none of it comes true.*

"You hear what I say?"

Moy's head came up sharply at her mother's demand. "Yes, I hear." She looked at her mother, her eyes wide with worry. She stared at Keem's white face. "Ma? You don't feel well?" Moy was quick on her feet, her small hands patting her mother's face.

"No. Why?" her mother asked, seeing her daughter's worried face.

"Your face white, white." Moy ran her hands gently over Keem's face. But her mother grabbed them and held them to her warm, soft chest.

"Listen to me, Moy. I already tell your grandpa about it, and I scare. I want you and Grandpa go to Thailand first. Then I follow after I sell our house and belonging."

"No!" Moy whispered, looking beyond her mother to the buses, taxis, and people on the busy streets. This was the only type of life she knew. And it was impossible to imagine it being destroyed.

It seemed to Moy people there in Pailin were very much like those in Siem Reap, where she had lived until she was seven. Everyone had some kind of business. Women not only kept house but cooked whatever they could—rice, pork with long green beans, and rice cakes to sell at the open-air market. Families often came to the market around 4:00 or 5:00 a.m. to get the best spot for their small, homemade tables or large cook pots. Some Khmer sold fish, vegetables, or live chickens or ducks. And some Chinese men sold pork or beef in the small stalls at the center of the market that had been built by the Khmer government. Vendors kept lowering prices to compete for customers, and occasionally, angry shouts filled the air as one accused another of stealing customers. At other times, all the vendors sold their goods at the same prices. And everyone would laugh and be friends again. Children as young as five or seven helped their families sell food or sold iced coffee or tea tied in small plastic bags from coolers on the sidewalk. But most people in Pailin sold lottery tickets and cigarettes on the sidewalks near the bus station, just as Keem did. Business was good because children as young as nine smoked. And everyone wanted to buy lottery tickets and get rich.

People in Pailin and Siem Reap dressed pretty much alike. In both cities, the Khmer women and Khmer men wore sarongs of various colors, while the Chinese women wore long, silky black pants. A few Chinese and Khmer men wore shorts, but most wore long pants all year round. While some Khmer men went shirtless in the summer, the more proper Chinese always clothed themselves from top to bottom in public. Khmer children up to the age of two or three generally went around naked. But the Chinese wouldn't let their children out of the house unless they were completely clothed. Most adult Khmers and some children wore plaid shawls around their heads, tied to one side or at the back of their heads to protect them from the hot sun, but the Chinese went bareheaded. On the other hand, most Khmer walked barefoot, while the Chinese, young or old, wore flip-flops.

In Siem Reap, with its paved streets and wide variety of clothing, shoe, and jewelry stores, people were generally cleaner than they were on the dirt roads of Pailin. But those who had succeeded in the local ruby and sapphire mining and trade were much richer than any in Siem Reap. Wealthy Pailin residents would buy their wives and daughters Western-style clothing.

Moy was so deep in thought that she forgot all about her mother's fears. *How could anything happen here, when people all around are laughing and yelling and a group of Khmer children are fighting over a piece of candy?*

"You hear what I say?"

"What?" Moy asked in confusion. She needed only one look at her mother's face to know she had hurt Keem deeply. Moy looked down at her hands, ashamed and guilty, and silently vowed that she would never let her beloved mother or grandfather down again, no matter what they wanted from her. It was a vow destined to be broken.

2
Love Is a
Poison Knife

...love?
Oh sweet love!
Dark like night, and
Cold like ice

Oh sweet love!
Deadly like a
Poison knife,

Love?
Oh sweet love...!

While the family had dinner that night, the nightmare began for Moy.

"Keem, I want you and Moy go Thailand first. After I sell house and all ciga-rette, I follow. See, if you can find us a house."

Moy interrupted her grandfather sharply. "I won't go! I'd rather live or die with Grandpa!" she screamed in a horrified voice.

"Then you go with Grandpa first and I go later," her mother proposed.

"I won't go with either of you!" Moy screamed again. Tears gathered in her eyes. She glanced quickly from her mother on the left to her grandfather on the right. In frustration, she shoved her rice bowl and chopsticks away so suddenly that she pushed the big bowl of pork soup against the wall and sent food spilling over the table, the floor, and their clothes.

No one moved or said a word. Then Grandpa Wong broke the silence. "If you dare do this again, I hit you hard!" Moy looked down at her place on the table, not knowing what to think or do, feeling helpless at her grandpa's threat.

"You listen to your ma. War here—"

"Even if there nothing to eat, but drink a bowl of water, I rather live or die with Ma!" Moy screamed. The thought of being parted from either of them was enough to send her soul out of her body. She looked sharply at her beloved grandpa as if to say, "You cannot do this to me!"

Wong took off his eyeglasses and rubbed his face as if to take the anger away. Then slowly, he replaced the eyeglasses on top of his nose. He looked long and hard at the mess on the table, caused by his headstrong granddaughter, as if trying to find a way to soften her hard head. Then he spoke in a low, clear voice, "You must go with your ma now. War here. Country become Communist if Black Shirts take over. It not take me long to sell—"

"I won't go. I drink a bowl of water, live or die with Grandpa!" Moy looked at both of them, her tearful eyes begging them not to make her leave without one of them. Couldn't they understand how she felt?

Wong and Keem looked at each other with a mixture of helplessness and pride. Their eyes seemed to say that they both knew how hard it would be to change the stubborn little girl's mind. They also seemed to realize why Moy had said what she did and felt proud of her loyalty to them. But neither would give up hope of changing Moy's mind. And in the weeks and months that followed, they tried often but unsuccessfully to reason with her.

Moy remembered only too well what it was like to be separated from one of them. When they were living in Siem Reap, Grandpa often took off on business trips to Phnom Penh to buy sugar, candy, rice, eggs, and cigarettes for their small five-and-dime shop. She remembered she always cried to go with him. He would pick her up, hug her, and lie, as Chinese adults did to children: "Grandpa only go buy sugar and thing. I come back tonight. Good child, don't cry." But he wouldn't return for a week or two. And Moy was always afraid he'd never come back. Many times, she would go kneel in front of the Earth Uncle's spirit stand and tearfully beg for her grandpa's safe return. She knelt so long her knees almost fell off, prayed so long her arms almost came away at the shoulders, and begged so loud she was almost toothless. When he finally returned, she felt like the sun had just been born and the earth created anew. And she bounded around like a puppy to welcome him home. Because business was good, he'd have to go off again a few days or a week later. And Moy would be in agony again.

Moy also remembered the good times she had missed when Grandpa was away, like going out for pork noodle soup every morning or riding on his motorcycle to the movies, to see his friends, or to visit the great Buddha temples at Angkor. Even the new dolls and toys he brought her from his trips couldn't make up for his absence.

And Ma…only last year, Ma had to go to Phnom Penh to get a new passport and ended up staying there for six months, after telling me it would be a week or two at the most. To be fair, it wasn't Ma's fault, but the Cambodian government's. Every government official wanted bribes. You give them ten ning; they want twenty. You give them twenty, they want a hundred. If they don't get what they want, they just make you wait and wait until they're sure you don't have any more money to give them, before they give you the passport. Chinese never get a fair deal in this unlucky country, Moy thought. *Look at the schools, for example. For the same class and teacher, the Chinese pay twenty thousand ning a year and the Cambodians only pay ten thousand. And Chinese students are punished a lot more, even when they give the right answer.* That was why Moy had gone to school only three months. Even though her family could afford the payment, she found there was no welcome at school for her, only regular beatings. One day, she couldn't even hold her hands up right. Her teacher had beaten them until they nearly bled. She remembered the pain on Keem's and Wong's faces. They cried, "My sad child!" Keem and Wong bought ice and put it on Moy's swollen hands. Keem had told Moy it was up to her whether she would go back to school and learn to read and write. Moy decided not to go back.

Keem often talked of saving enough money so they could all go live in Hong Kong, among Chinese people. And Moy often daydreamed about this. But it would be Keem's nightmare and not Moy's daydream that would come true.

3
Friend or
Enemy

The first time you saw a shark
You thought it was your friend
But you couldn't see his
Teeth.

When you saw a dolphin swim off
Shore
You thought it was your enemy,
Because you saw his
Fin.

Sometime in April of 1975, the nightmare became real. One night, as Moy and her family were having dinner at their usual time of 10:00 p.m., suddenly, they heard loud screams from the streets. Moy's mother and grandfather froze, their rice bowls and chopsticks right under their noses. Moy's lips on the bowl and the chopsticks in her mouth, she looked at her mother and grandfather with big eyes.

"Why people yell?" Keem asked, still holding the rice bowl under her mouth.

"Maybe Black Shirt come," Wong said, putting down his bowl and chopsticks.

"We go see them?" Moy asked the chopsticks still in her mouth.

Her mother gave her a hard look, but Grandpa said, "Eat fast if you want to go." At that, Moy started to push the rice into her mouth as fast as she could. She heard Keem and Wong let out a long breath, as if to say, "What are we going to do with her?"

"I full!" Moy announced with a grin, putting her bowl down, but her mother gave her an angry look.

"Eat another bowl."

"I full."

"Eat more!"

"She full. How can she eat more?"

"You spoil her, Dad."

"And you?" Wong asked his daughter, grinning as he looked at her rice bowl, still half full.

Keem looked down at the bowl and then back at Wong. "You spoil her and always take her side."

"Ha!" Wong smiled handsomely. He looked at Moy and then asked, "She say I spoil you. Do I?"

"No!" Moy grinned back.

"I never see grandfather and granddaughter more alike."

"She angry. You eat more."

"I full."

"Then go wash bowl and wait till your ma finish. She go with you."

"Me? You take her."

"I old, and I want to stay home." Wong smiled sweetly at his daughter, got up, and went into the kitchen.

The street was quiet as Moy and her mother walked along it. The closer they got to the main street, the louder the screams of excitement from the people became. Hundreds and hundreds of people lined the sidewalks. Keem and Moy joined them and looked up toward the hill. They saw a big line of four-door cars coming toward the crowd.

"Who is it?" Moy asked in Khmer to the nearest person.

"Khmer Red." This was the Cambodian way of referring to the Khmer Rouge.

"That not Khmer Red," said the man next to Keem. "That governor of Battambang and all his soldier. They flee to Thailand before Khmer Red get here."

"Khmer Red in Phnom Penh now. They come to Pailin soon," a Cambodian woman put in from behind the man. (Phnom Penh was the capital of Cambodia.)

"Governor intelligent," someone said in Khmer from the other side of Moy. "He not wait till Khmer Red come to cut his throat."

"If I have car, I go too!" someone else said.

"What you worry about? There be peace when Khmer Red come in. No more fighting!" a man screamed from somewhere.

"That just talk. You not know anything!" a woman yelled back.

"We go home, Moy," Keem whispered. But Moy's ears were standing up like a rabbit's. She didn't want to miss anything. Her eyes grew larger and larger with so much to see. It was like New Year's Day to her. "We go home." Her mother spoke louder this time and started to pull Moy's arm.

"Little later," Moy pulled her arm from her mother's grasp, not even looking at her. Her small head was bobbing up and down as she tried to see the road between people's shoulders. But she was too short and too far back.

"We go home, now!" Her mother pulled harder on her arm. Seeing Keem's angry face, Moy did as she was told.

Two or three days later, the first Khmer Rouge came to Pailin very late at night. Some people saw them take down the Cambodian flag in front of the old store on the main street and replace it with a white one. The next morning, Moy awoke with a start around seven o'clock, surprised not to find her mother in bed next to her.

"Ma?"

"Sun shine at your butt, now you wake up." She heard her mother laugh softly from the dinner table.

"Sky almost fall down and her eye just open," she heard her grandfather tease. "Come eat," Grandpa told her. Moy went to stand by her mother, rubbing her sleepy eyes with the backs of her hands, like she was still four years old. "So little!" Grandpa teased. And Moy played for attention by dropping her hands and trying her best to look like a tiny, helpless puppy. Before she could ask anything, her mother told her to wash her face and then eat if she wanted to go see the Khmer Rouge.

She finished washing and eating in ten minutes, and all three people were on their way to town. The main street was crowded with Chinese and Khmer men, women, and children—even tiny babies lined up to welcome the Khmer Rouge. There was music from cymbals, drums, and flutes. Some Chinese men played the "Eight Angels Song," the song used to wish people good luck, peace, and success at weddings and birthdays. Cambodian men, women, and children were also dancing and singing in Khmer. People along the sidewalks shouted, "Success Khmer Red!" and waved pieces of white cloth in the air, as if letting the Khmer Rouge know they had surrendered to them. The shouts of the crowd grew louder as the Khmer Rouge came down the hill, car after car and truck after truck. The bands moved on to the sidewalks. The singers sang louder, and the drumbeaters beat harder.

All the Khmer Rouge men, women, and children were dressed in black with red plaid shawls around their necks. They smiled, showing off their white teeth; they waved and called everyone, "Buddy," as their cars and trucks went by. They all looked warm and friendly. But soon, Moy would find out how deceptive a smile could be.

4

That day, when the Khmer Rouge first came, no one in Pailin did any business. People soon went back to their normal routine, but there were differences. Prices dropped sharply. A bowl of pork noodle soup that had previously cost fifty ning now cost one. The rich ruby and sapphire buyers put all their paper money into large rice bags and took them to the police station for safekeeping.

The Khmer Rouge kept to themselves for a day or two but then made their presence felt. First of all, they were too familiar, calling everyone "buddy," even a fifty-year-old woman, which was considered rude and disrespectful. The Chinese and Khmer always addressed their elders as "Grandpa" or "Grandma," in respect for their maturity. More frightening was the way the Khmer Rouge always had people looking over their shoulders, not just in public but at home too. The Khmer Rouge would show up on the streets with long guns over their shoulders. They would smile and chat and call people "Buddy." Then they would demand people's belongings. Watches, jewelry, whatever they laid their eyes on and wanted, they would take. After all, they had guns. They would just walk into someone's house for dinner, sometimes one person, sometimes a group. At first, people felt sorry for them, because they had just come from a war, and people would feed them. But the next day, the Khmer Rouge would show up at the same house, with a larger group for dinner.

At the stores, the Khmer Rouge would eat whatever they pleased and then say, "Thanks, buddy," and walk off without paying. They took vendors' cigarettes the same way, not just one pack but two or three. Day after day of this abuse hurt people's businesses. Sometimes, a group of them filled the entire pork noodle soup shop. And when they left, another group took their place. Not a penny went to the shop for the whole day. They took clothing, shoes, and other things from the shops, whenever they liked. Day by day, people became more and more afraid of the Khmer Rouge.

What they did in people's homes was even more frightening. The Khmer Rouge just walked into people's houses and asked for their belongings. If people refused, the Khmer Rouge took them anyway. They took knives, clothes, radios, sewing machines, bicycles, motorcycles, and cars—whatever they wanted. If people resisted, they would be beaten or kicked, young and old alike. This was how the soldiers, the "protectors of the innocent," treated the people of Pailin.

The real nightmare began in the second week. One morning, around 4:00 a.m., angry voices filled the streets of Pailin. Every radio station carried the same message from Onka, the Khmer Rouge government: "Buddy Sister, Buddy Brother, Buddy Father, and Buddy Mother, Onka decide to evacuate you from our city for three day to get rid of all our enemy. Take what you can carry. After three day, buddy sister, buddy brother, buddy father, and buddy mother can return to your hometown." At first, people thought it was a hoax, and about noon, Onka announced on the radio: "Buddy Sister, Buddy Brother, Buddy Father, and Buddy Mother, Onka sorry for mistake Onka make earlier. Now Onka decide not to evacuate you."

But the people's joy didn't last, because two or three hours later, the radio broadcast the first announcement again. For the next three days, the two announcements were alternated until no one knew what to think. Then on the fourth day, there was a new announcement: "Buddy Sister, Buddy Brother, Buddy Father, and Buddy Mother, Onka say if you have farm, you don't have to leave. If you not have farm, Onka want you to evacuate your home. If you not leave, you responsible for what happen. Onka want everyone out of city by April 30."

Everyone prayed and hoped that Onka would change its mind. But their prayers were not answered, and the nightmare didn't go away. The last two or three days before the deadline, people went to the stores to buy whatever food and goods they could lay their hands on. Every family was busy finding a wagon or two to carry their belongings, or at least their food. People who couldn't find a wagon, like Moy's second uncles, made their own out of boards, with hand-carved wooden wheels.

5

Before they left Pailin, Moy and her mother went to the store for a final look around. The store was small, with a mud floor that got everyone dirty when it rained, but no one ever complained. By this time on a normal morning, the shop would be busy, but on this day, it was empty. Keem's cigarette table was missing from its spot in the far right corner. And there were no buses with people reaching down to buy cigarettes from them.

Moy looked around sadly at the empty store. It was located in a busy area of the main street in between two side streets filled with small houses of the same size and height. In most of these houses, the owner lived in back and had a shop in the front. Moy loved to watch these shops, which were usually bustling with customers. There were shops that sold candy, comic books, and toys; a bakery; and a barbershop. Today, as she looked at the empty street and the locked wooden doors of the shops, it seemed to her as if the signs above the shops, once intended for human eyes, now stared only at the cement, waiting for the dust and dirt to cover them.

Across the main street from the store was the small, blue wooden police station, looking strangely bare without the cars that usually surrounded it. The station was located in the left corner of a large park, where ruby and sapphire traders met to do business. On a normal day, the park would be filled with traders on their motorcycles or on foot and the sounds of their loud voices. Farther down, you would hear the laughter of children as they played on the swings or slides while their parents did business. But today…the park was deserted.

From Keem's cigarette table, Moy would watch the schoolchildren in their white shirts and dark-blue skirts or pants, as they went to and from the Cambodian school. Today, the peals of their laughter and the scuffle of their flip-flops were only a memory.

Higher up the hill, the main street was always crowded with patrons of the pork noodle shops and with people waiting to get into the movie theater. Today, the theater doors were closed and the only people on the sidewalks had sad faces. They were quiet as they looked at the places they were going to leave behind. Moy tried to imagine what the empty theater looked like without the colorful images and laughter that usually filled it; she tried to picture the blank white screen, the prison-like cement walls that shut out all the light, and the empty wooden seats. *Is this what the life of Pailin will be like from now on?*

As the day neared when they had to leave, the voice inside Moy's heart was unclear. She didn't know what it was saying to her. On the last day, she walked around the house, taking a final and careful look. It was a big house made of brown wood with a cement floor and thin metal roof. The kitchen was in a tiny room, with the toilet only about three feet away. But the fact that the toilet was indoors and the house had a cement floor showed the family's middle-class status. In the main room, Moy and Keem's bed was against one wall, with a tall chest at the foot and a shelf full of cigarettes at the head. A flowered orange curtain surrounded the bedroom area, separating it from the rest of the room. To the left of the bedroom, against the kitchen wall, was the round dinner table, with her grandpa's chair in the corner to the left. Her mother's chair was to the right, by the entrance to the kitchen. And Moy's chair was in the middle. Grandpa's folding bed was against the opposite wall from their bedroom, next to the front door. Against the walls were a few metal chairs, three or four huge bags of rice, and Moy's toys. Moy felt sad about walking out and leaving so many things behind—clothes, food, toys—but there was no choice.

Moy walked out and stood in front of the house, looking at the cement well and the big tree next to it. Two or three feet from the well were the sugar canes Keem had planted for Moy. They were just about a foot high.

"I grow that sugar cane for you to eat, because you like it so much. Now it look like someone else eat it for you." Keem laughed softly and sadly behind Moy.

It's so hard to chew but so sweet to taste. But all for nothing, Moy thought, looking long and hard at the sugar cane. *So hard and sweet, but all for nothing...just like life.*

By the twenty-ninth, only about half the people had left Pailin. The rest stayed, hoping Onka would change their mind. But nothing changed, and on the thirtieth, almost everyone was out of the city. Moy's family left that day, April 30, 1975, carrying what they could on her second uncle's homemade wagon.

6

Moy and her mother met her grandpa and her second uncle at the corner of the main road and the long street leading to their houses. With their belongings on their shoulders, they joined the thousands of others along the main road—people whose whole lives had been reduced to what they could carry with them. As people walked toward Battambang, some laughed. As if there were still some hope of finding a way to destroy the great hammer that threatened to break their hearts. But their eyes were filled with sorrow, and tears of despair rolled down their cheeks.

Everyone—young and old; woman, man, and child—was on the road. They welcomed the burning sun above to numb their brains. They welcomed the scorching earth below to numb their hearts. They welcomed the sweat running down their backs to wash away their sad memories. Each step forward was a step away from the safe and familiar. Old and young alike—even the tiniest babies—shared this first pain of exile. There was no mercy anywhere, not even from the sweet wind. The air was heavy and still, and the cruel heat turned their knees to water. But their feet would not give in. Their dry lips and throats cried out for water, but there was nothing along the road but trees, dry earth, and sand. They did find water in a small pond, but there was a body floating facedown in it. Moy saw each arm was about half a foot in diameter and a sickening gray color. The clothing on the body was torn. They were too small for the bloated body. People overlooked the dead body and drank the water anyway.

Old or young, all did their share. Some carried bundles of clothing and food wrapped in sarongs on their shoulders. Others pulled or pushed wagons full of their belongings. Everyone who could walk walked. The very old and the very young who could not walk either sat on top of the bundles in the wagons or were carried by family members on their backs—people who were already burdened with food and clothing. Some people had boxes or bags, one in front and the other behind, slung over their shoulders on carry sticks and tied on with ropes, the bigger boxes or bags for adults and the smaller boxes and bags for the nine- or ten-year-olds. The little children carried little things like bowls or spoons and walked next to their parents.

Hour after hour, there was nothing to see but trees and the long, empty road ahead. Sometimes people stopped under a roadside tree or went a little deeper into the forest to cook a meal. They dug a hole in the ground and made a cooking fire with leaves and branches. Some people slept or rested beneath the trees or under the wagons, which had pulled into the forest to allow others to pass.

Before the Khmer Rouge came, the road had been used for the buses and taxis that connected Pailin to Battambang and other places. But now, there were no cars, taxis, or buses—just human feet and wagon wheels on the tearstained road. When people dropped from weariness, there was the hard earthen bed to welcome them and the sky for a roof. Sometimes, the sky was so friendly, it sent the rain down in the middle of the night, concerned that people's skin might be too dry. If they felt lonely, their good friends the *mosquitoes* were there to keep them company day or night, seven days a week. In spite of the adults' pain, the two- and three-year-olds ran and played and screamed with laughter. They ate and slept, as if they wouldn't care if the whole world came down on their heads.

On the third or fourth day on the road, as she and her mother slept under a tree next to the wagon, Moy was suddenly awakened by a scream of pain. She sat up slowly and looked for her mother, but Keem wasn't there. Looking around, she saw her grandpa near his older son's family. They were all asleep on the other side of the wagon. Grandpa sat alone, leaning against the wooden wagon wheel and smoking a cigarette, as if nothing was bothering him. In the darkness, Moy could see only his white, short-sleeved shirt. And once in a while, she saw the side of his sad face, as the tip of his cigarette brightened. He sat with his knees drawn up, deep in thought, as if no pain could reach him.

Again, she heard a scream of pain from the other side of the road. But everything looked normal. Most people were sleeping; some were waving their hands back and forth, chasing the mosquitoes away, and others were lying still, even though the mosquitoes must have been eating them alive. Some people sat alone like Grandpa, deep in thought. A small group was gathered near a fire, smoking, talking, and laughing sadly or just quietly staring at the flames. Others walked over to join the group or tried to clear their minds by pacing back and forth near their wagons or wandering among the helpless sleepers.

Moy looked down at her feet, searching for a way to bring back to all these people what they had lost and make them all happy again. But she was as helpless as everyone else. She looked up slowly at the black sky and the bright moon. *Black and white, nothing in between,* she thought.

"Grandpa?" She had to say it twice before he answered.

"Mmm?" His head turned sharply toward her voice. "What? Why you not sleep?"

Moy didn't answer right away but went to sit between his knees, her small back leaning against his big chest. His free arm wrapped around her. "Why you not sleep like others, Grandpa?"

"I can't sleep."

"You worry?"

"No, I not worry."

"That good," she whispered sadly. "Grandpa, where Ma go?"

"She..." He sounded uncomfortable. Moy turned in his big arm to look at his face. "She help...mmm...baby."

"Huh?" Moy cocked her head to one side and looked at his face, but he turned away from her. When she heard another painful scream, this one definitely female, Moy demanded again, "Grandpa?"

"Go see! Don't ask so much!" Wong snapped angrily at his granddaughter.

Moy jumped, drawing away from him. He let her go from his big arm. She walked to the other side of the road where she found a large group of women. Standing behind them, she began to understand what the screaming was about. She stared at a Cambodian girl, about sixteen or seventeen, who was trying to give birth. Sweat rolled down the girl's forehead. She bit down hard on a balled-up shirt. Her strong white teeth showed against the dark sleeve that hung from one side of her mouth. Her face was covered with tears and sweat. She kept thrusting her head back and forth but couldn't stop moaning from the pain. She was giving birth in the middle of the night, in the middle of nowhere. The earth was her bed and the sky her roof. There was no privacy, no doctor, not even any water. Every time she cried out, her eyes grew wider with pain and helplessness. The older women tried to help her in any way they could, by speaking softly to her, or smoothing her black hair from her forehead. *How sad,* Moy thought. *She should have a better place than this to give birth...*

"What you do here?"

Before she knew what was happening, Moy found herself being pulled away in her mother's angry grasp. Trembling behind her mother, Moy tried to explain, "Grandpa say—"

"Grandpa! Grandpa! Everything Grandpa!" Keem spoke in anger, pulling her daughter behind her across the road. "You want to see everything! Understand everything! And if you not hear and know everything, you can't sit still or stand still, like worm eat your butt!"

Moy giggled at her mother's last statement, and Keem stopped, furious. They both nearly fell over when Moy bumped into her.

"Ooo!" Moy's free hand covered her mouth as she peeked at her mother's face.

Keem yanked her daughter around to face her, shaking a finger under Moy's nose, speaking in a hard tone. "You this big and still act like silly little girl!"

Moy couldn't stop giggling and turned to look at her backside. "Worm eat my butt, but it still good, good!" Moy struggled in Keem's grasp, turning to show her bottom to her mother. "See?" she asked in a playful voice, pulling her small face into an expression of pure innocence. She got a light, playful kick on her backside for a response.

"This one!" Keem looked away, yanking her daughter along with her. But Moy could see her mother's shoulders shaking with laughter. *You don't want me to see you laugh. But I know you too well for that,* Moy thought with a grin.

7

People lost count of the endless days on the road toward Battambang. They walked before the new sun was born each day and stopped to eat when they got hungry. They slept when their eyes would not stay open. One day, Moy was eating lunch with her mother beside their wagon when she heard a group of Khmer speaking in terrified voices. The group was close enough for her to hear every word. A Cambodia man told his story.

His family and other families were waiting about two kilometers outside of Pailin for three days. They went back like the Khmer Rouge told them. When they got to the hill that led into Pailin from Battambang Road, the Khmer Rouge asked why they came back. People told them that Onka said after three days they could return. And the Khmer Rouge told them Onka didn't want people in the city anymore. When people didn't move fast enough, the Khmer Rouge started shooting people with their machine guns! That man's family was at the back, and he lost one daughter. The families in front were killed by the Khmer Rouge's machine guns. They didn't shoot the young girls. They took the girls and raped them. Someone asked the girl's father if he saw that happen.

The man said he saw the Khmer Red shoot people right in front of him. But they didn't shoot the young girls, just older people. They pulled and dragged all the young girls away before they shot their families. The young girls were screaming and crying. His daughter was in front with her friend's family, and the Khmer Red dragged her away. He asked people to tell him if the Khmer Red didn't rape those girls, then why did they pull them away from their families and not shoot them? No one answered.

The man told the story sobbing loudly. Moy saw him wipe tears off his face with the back of his hand. She could see only one side of his long, bony face. She guessed he was about forty or fifty. He went on.

30

"My daughter fight Khmer Red soldier…and he hit her with his gun." The man was crying harder and had trouble going on with his tale of horror. "She get up and run…hold her head in her hand and scream, 'Father, run! Father, run!'… and they…shot her in the back! Why Khmer kill Khmer? My own Khmer people kill my daughter, who speak Khmer like them!" The man went on crying, and the others tried to ease his pain.

Someone spoke to him in Khmer, "That child know what Khmer Red want to do with her. She run to be shot, so they not rape her. She go to Buddha now and not suffer like us."

A horror story like this, no one would ever forget. It was real life, not a movie. People might not talk about it, but it would be there in their hearts and minds, reminding them of what was in store for them. If Khmers killed Khmers, what would the Black Shirts do to the Chinese and the others? If the Black Shirts had no mercy on their own dark-skinned people, who spoke the same language as they did, what kind of mercy would they give to people not like them? What did one do when one has seen blood and death in person? It seemed life must go on.

So life did go on, and soon, the travelers found out what the Khmer Rouge had in mind for them. At the small town between Pailin and Battambang, everyone was stopped by the Khmer Rouge. The road was blocked by piles and piles of bicycles, motorcycles, cars, and buses that had been torn apart, even the brand-new ones—trunks in one pile, doors in another, and so forth, all in two long lines. On the left was a large brown wooden house, about thirty feet long, with a metal roof and a large front porch with two steps leading up to it. On the right was a group of similar brown wooden houses that had had the doors removed and the walls knocked down. They had made them into one long house for everyone to live in.

The Khmer Rouge made everyone stop and sit on the road between the two houses. Everyone waited in terror. Would the Khmer Rouge use their machine guns on the men, women, and babies? Would they rape young girls in front of their parents? The worst was the waiting. But in about a half hour, one of the Khmer Rouge appeared on the porch of the house on the left, holding a megaphone. His skin was dark, almost black, and his black hair was combed back from his face. He wore long pants and a long-sleeved shirt of black cotton with a plaid shawl around his neck and a pair of black shoes with soles made from tire treads and straps from bicycle tires. *Do all the Black Shirts wear the same shoes?* Moy looked around. *Sure enough, every one of them! Why didn't I notice that before? Because I was too busy watching their friendly faces and their white teeth!* Moy thought. *Now what does this Black Shirt have to say to us?* The same question was in everyone's mind.

The Black Shirt came down stiffly from the stairs, head held high. And the crowd nearly forgot to let out their breath. They had been holding it so long. He turned very slowly to look at everyone, as if he were afraid he would lose a bone or two if he moved any faster. Holding the megaphone to his mouth, he showed his white teeth in a cold smile and then started to speak to his "buddies." He told everyone to rest in the long house or on the road for the night. Everyone would be given rice and salt the next day. He told the crowd Onka had a town about two hours away, where they would go and live. Onka would provide them all with food. He ended by shouting, "Success Community Cambodia!" raising his right fist high. All the Khmer Rouge did the same, raised their guns in their hands. Then he told the crowd to shout the same words and raise their fists. No one talked much or did much that night, except to get water from the community well for drinking or bathing. Some people slept in the long house, but most slept in the road. The gray concrete floor of the house was stained dark brown. And the house smelled of mud, blood, and other things—no one knew exactly what.

The next morning, the Khmer Rouge gave out rice and salt, as promised. People stood in line, and each family received sixty cans (the size of a small soup can) of rice and four or five cans of salt, "For now." As soon as each family got their food, the Khmer Rouge made them leave for the town in the forest, telling them to come back if they needed more food.

The road into the jungle was only a footpath about six feet wide, with the tall grass worn away by the feet of the people who had come earlier. The road was mostly brown soil with large and small rocks all over, which made it hard to pull the wagons along. The rocks cut through people's bare feet or thin flip-flops as they walked. But they didn't care so much about their bleeding feet, because the Khmer man's horror story was still burning in their minds.

Farther on, the road became brown or black mud that made walking and pulling the wagons more and more difficult. Sometimes, the mud was ankle deep or higher. People tried to help each other. But sometimes it was almost impossible, since the mud holes became bigger and deeper when people tried to push the stuck wagons out. Some slipped and fell in the mud, taking bundles of clothes and food with them. Bending down to free a flip-flop stuck in the mud, others would find their bags on their shoulders and heads and tumble into the puddles and muck. If the bags were big enough, the unlucky people might find themselves trapped facedown in the mud. But others always stopped to help. Wagon owners sometimes thanked people who helped them by offering to carry some of their belongings on the wagon. People made new friends this way. They would then stop to have lunch or dinner together and talk about living next to each other in the new town.

But no matter how long they walked, they found no town—only trees and long grass. Some people found a small footpath to the right and decided to follow it, while the rest went straight. By four or five in the afternoon, most people had to stop to rest on the wet ground. Those who had waterproof materials put them down first to keep their clothes dry. They sat and thought about their future, but what kind of future would it be? As far as they could see, there were only the forest and the mountains in the distance.

All of Wong's children and grandchildren stopped together. The men rested, while the women and children went to find wood for a fire. Each family found three big rocks, which they formed into a cooking stove, and gathered enough dry wood to make a fire. The problem was they didn't have any water. But soon, Moy and some of the others found water in a big rut in the road, which had been made by the wheels of a truck. Everyone took a rice can full of water, being careful to draw the clearer water from the top. If someone dipped too deep and stirred up the mud, the water would look like coffee with milk in it. The others would yell at that person to be more careful. Then everyone had to wait till the mud settled again to get some more water. Then they put each can full of water into a larger pot. Everyone did the same, rich or poor, Chinese and Khmer alike. And everyone knew then that their food and their lives would never be the same again.

8

"Why rice taste like mud?" Moy wanted to know.

"Water come from mud, rice taste like mud!" her mother answered sweetly.

"Don't bite too big on fry pork. When we finish that, we not have any more," Wong told his granddaughter softly.

They sat crowded together on a piece of green plastic to keep dry. For dinner, each had a bowl of rice and a small piece of pork. Moy held the small piece of brown meat with her chopsticks, examining it carefully as she chewed her food. She asked, as if she didn't already know the answer, "Where we sleep tonight?" She put the piece of pork back in the rice bowl and peered at their faces.

Wong and Keem looked at each other, as if she were out of her mind to ask the question. Wong put down his bowl and chopsticks and laughed loudly.

"Here where we sleep tonight, child," he said through his laughter. He looked at the sky and said to no one in particular, "The moon bright, bright." With that, he picked up the bowl and chopsticks and began eating again.

"We see what people do, then we follow," Keem put in as she chewed her food.

"If they jump down from mountain, you jump too?" Wong asked.

"Then what we do?"

"We see what people do, then we judge. If it good, we follow. If not, we don't."

"What happen if everyone leave and you think that bad? We just stay here all alone?" Keem asked.

"People keep come in. We not alone."

"Grandpa, let me give you more rice."

"I full!"

"Don't interrupt!" Keem snapped at her daughter.

"Listen to your father's word," Wong told Keem.

I don't like this, Moy thought, looking at the frowns on both their faces. "Why you argue? I just ask where we sleep," she asked.

"Don't interrupt when older people talk!" Keem snapped.

"You two not talk, you argue."

"You very stubborn!" Wong shouted angrily at his granddaughter.

Moy put down her rice bowl and chopsticks and started to cry quietly. She felt hurt to be attacked by the two people who loved her more than their own lives. It was not that they never punished her when she was too stubborn to listen. They did hit her with long thin sticks, like most Chinese parents did. But only once had they really beaten her badly. And she would never forget it. When she was six, she stole twenty ning and went out to a movie with fifteen or twenty poor Chinese and Cambodian kids, who were several years older.

She felt sorry for them because their parents were too poor to buy enough food for them, and they had talked her into taking the money. But she ran short, and one of the Cambodian boys couldn't go in with them. He threatened to tell her parents if she didn't take him too. He was as good as his word, she remembered. Wong and Keem had taken turns hitting her. It seemed like it went on for hours. They beat her until the sticks broke. Then they went to find new ones and beat her again until she couldn't cry or scream or even feel the pain anymore. They hit her until she just sat there tiny and frightened, her hands waving back and forth protecting her small helpless body, face, and head.

She also remembered they had shouted shameful words at her while they beat her, and she had cried with pain, "I dare not do it again, Ma, Grandpa! I dare not do it again!" But they had no mercy.

They didn't stop until an older woman next door yelled from the roofless common kitchen, "You not hit her enough yet? Hit her as a listen-teaching. But you hit her till she die! Don't you hear? That child can't cry anymore. What kind of people you? Even animal have mercy on their child. Not you! Why not take knife and cut her throat if you that angry?"

"You very mean hit that child like that." A Cambodian woman living next door on the other side spoke up. Her husband worked for the Cambodian government. "Teach child, not kill child, when child do wrong. Put them in jail for hit that child like that!" she told her husband.

"Hit her enough yet? Is that child die? I not hear her cry anymore," the husband asked. "Mean, mean mother and grandfather, that child have."

Afterward, Moy's eyes had been so swollen she couldn't open them for nearly a week. She spent weeks in bed with a fever, because of the punishment, Moy also remembered. Her mother had cried very hard each time she came to rub the Chinese ointment on Moy's wounds or give her medicine to drink to relieve the swelling. "Ma sorry, child, Ma sorry!" Keem sobbed aloud; shameful tears dripped and dripped from her eyes. "My child, my pulse, my flesh, my life, my child, Ma sorry!" Then Keem would get off the bed and go kneel in front of Great-Grandma's and Great-Grandpa's spirit stands on top of the dresser. She would tearfully beg Great-Grandma and Great-Grandpa not to let anything happen to Moy. "I dare not hit her again, Grandma and Grandpa. I dare not. Save my child. I beg you, Grandma and Grandpa. I beg you. I wrong; Dad wrong. My child is my life. Please save my child." Keem did this every day until Moy was back to health again.

And Grandpa brought her bright-colored, sweet-flavored ice balls three or four times a day, even though he normally didn't approve of her eating the artificial colors. Moy also remembered Keem and Wong cooked a whole chicken, rice, and other foods and prayed to thank Great-Grandma and Great-Grandpa's sprits for helping Moy get healthy again. (Sometimes, there is more love in an iron fist...than a tender kiss.)

Never after that did Grandpa hit her with a stick. Though once, he had beaten her so hard on her little backside that Keem yelled at him to stop before he did her serious harm. Since that time, he had never hit her again. He threatened but didn't carry out the threat. Keem was the same way. But even though they didn't hit her, she still felt pain and horror when they got this angry with her.

"You dare cry?"

"Ma, I dare not do it again!" Moy screamed in a horrified voice.

"Keem, don't yell at her!" Wong shouted. "We eat and rest."

And everyone did just that, though Moy cried enough tears that they softened the rice in her bowl, which made it go down her small throat easier.

Moy lay down to sleep beside her mother on the green plastic, but she couldn't stop the tears from coming. The sky was clear, with a bright moon and thousands of stars twinkling down. The leaves on the trees danced around making strange noises. Moy heard sounds around the jungle that she had never heard before. Animals called out to each other angrily. *Who wouldn't be angry, if they were being forced out from their home? Black Shirts forced us out from our hometown. Now the animals think we are forcing them out of their homes, and they are angry.*

36

"You cold?" Keem asked her daughter, turning to wrap an arm around Moy before she could answer.

Moy kept her back to her mother and wiped tears off her face with the back of her hand; she whispered, "No."

"You can't sleep?" Keem drew her stubborn daughter closer.

"Yes."

"In Pailin, I scare if door not lock by ten o'clock at night. But now…I not scare. You think that strange?" Keem asked but got no response from her daughter. She rose up on one elbow and peered down at Moy's face; to her delight, she got a smile. "Flat-nosed lady!" She patted her daughter's small nose and whispered softly to the back of her head, "Go to sleep." And sleep did come for Moy…with no bad dreams.

9

The next day, everyone was busy finding a place to live. About four in the afternoon, Moy saw Grandpa with his three sons returning from the west. At dinner, he told Moy and Keem there was a small river to the west that would give them water, if they wanted to live there. But the land there was mostly sand and rocks. Here was a better place to grow crops, except for the lack of water. Wong had timed the trip with his watch. It took about four hours round-trip from there to the small river. Everyone had to think hard about which was more important—water or good land. After three days, the oldest son and the second son and their families, the fourth son, the third and the youngest daughters, and Wong's wife went to the west. Wong, the third son, Keem, and Moy stayed where they were.

For the first three or four weeks, the men built houses while the women went back to the big brown house in town for rice and salt. The Khmer Rouge was easy and friendly, but each time, they gave people less rice and salt. The men building the houses never had time to rest. The younger men cut down the larger trees, and the older men cut the smaller ones. They used any tools they had—carving knives, saws, and axes. It was much harder than they had expected. And small families had an especially hard time getting their areas cleared.

After a few days, everyone met and talked; they agreed to work together. If they cut down all the trees in one area and then moved to a new area, the work would go faster. That way, they all got to have a roof over their heads sooner. Women, children, older men, and older women cut the tall grass with knives and sickles. The work was easier for people from farms than for the city dwellers. In her whole eleven years, Moy had never even seen a sickle, but now they were everywhere.

Moy worked beside her mother, learning from watching Keem. She bent halfway down like Keem did, her left hand grasping the grass and right hand struggling to cut it with the small, dull knife. It was very hard.

"Don't grasp too much. Cut little, little, and don't cut your fingers!" Keem told her daughter in a worried voice.

"Yes." Moy smiled at her mother. "Why we cut grass? What we do with it?"

"If people cut grass, we cut grass." Keem paused and put down the grass in her hand. "Those square-stomach Khmer say, tie grass to small stick with root, then use it to cover roof of house. Like some square stomach house in Pailin." Keem looked at her daughter. "Use your eye; see how square stomach tie grass. Learn from them, so we can do it ourselves. It not easy ask people help." Keem got no response from her daughter, who seemed to be either too busy or having too much fun, attacking the tall green grass with the small knife. The grass was at least a foot taller than the little girl. From time to time, she cocked her head to one side and rubbed her cheek or ear with her wrist. Keem wondered if her daughter was having fun.

I'd rather be selling bread and lucky tickets than cutting this awful grass, Moy thought bitterly. *It makes everything itch…my arms, my hands, my feet, my body, my face, and my ears!*

But everyone else, the Chinese or Khmer, sounded so happy, talking and laughing. The Khmer would tease the Chinese to say something in Khmer. And when they didn't get it quite right, both would laugh. They teased and laughed back and forth. Sometimes, Keem and Moy heard the men laughing on the other side and wondered what they were laughing about. Some would joke that the men were talking about their love lives, and everyone would laugh. Some women shouted to their husbands to ask what they were laughing about. The men would shout back that women were always wondering what men were thinking. Or the husbands would say someone else's wife was more beautiful than theirs. Some husbands told their wives, "You old. I go marry young, beautiful wife." Then the jealous wives would throw down their tools, march angrily to the other side of the field, and beat their husbands. And everyone would stop to enjoy the show. Everyone would laugh as jealous wives chased their husbands around the field. The husbands would call out that they needed to find younger wives who wouldn't beat them.

The bolder Khmer wives would scream, "My back nearly broke because I cook rice and wash clothes for big penis! How dare he say I mean and old! Go find beautiful wife! She no cook food for big penis like you!" (Chinese wives wouldn't dare use such unladylike language!)

And the husbands would say, "Sound like my wife jealous!"

The work was hard, but everyone tried to have as much fun as they could.

In the daytime, the jungle was filled with the sounds of knives, axes, saws, falling trees, and human laughter. But at night, there was silence, sorrow, and fear. Seven days a week, men cut trees and women and children cut grass. As they worked, they were entertained by the mock fighting between wives and husbands. Sometimes, the mock fights turned into huge battles, when everyone attacked each other with leaves and grass. But that evening, people would cry themselves silently to sleep, worrying what would become of their children, in a place with only trees, grass, and wild animals. All they knew was that when the next day came, they would cut more trees and grass.

Once enough trees were down, the men began cutting them into the lengths they wanted and sorting them into piles. The women sprayed water on the dry brown grass, dampened the roots they had cut in water, and began tying them to the small sticks until the sticks were full and ready to be used to make a roof. Some men began digging holes with whatever tools they had for the walls of a house. Then they would set the tree trunks upright in the holes, one next to the other. Then the women and children would take over next, using their hands and feet to press the soil tight to hold the tree trunks upright. Inside the house, the men dug holes and set in shorter trunks to form the legs of a bed. The women laid smaller trunks side by side across them and tied them together with roots to make a bed. The sticks bound with grass were then tied together to make a roof. If anyone had any plastic material, it was tied to the inside of the walls to keep out the wind and rain.

Each day, the Khmer Rouge would come on their bicycles, flashing their white teeth and calling out to people, "Good work!" or, "You work very hard and faster than we expect." When the houses were almost done, the Khmer Rouge met with everyone and gave each family some private land to grow whatever vegetables they wanted for their own use. "And Onka can take them, if Onka need them," but no one else could use that land or take the vegetables. If they did, Onka would "hit you away" (kill them). But all the rest would be common and could only be used with the Onka government's permission. Then the Khmer Rouge divided the town into blocks: Block One, Block Two, etc. Some blocks had more families, some less; Moy's block had about ten or twelve families. Each block had a headman, who was the leader of the whole block, and a headwoman, who was the leader of the women who worked in the fields. The headman would go to town every week to pick up rice, salt, or meat for the block. In the common fields, the headman worked with the other men and told them which areas to work. The children worked with the women. Everyone worked side by side, Chinese or Khmer, rich or poor.

10

Moy's third uncle and his wife shared the same private land with Moy, Keem, and Wong. They all worked to cut down the trees on that land. Moy's two young cousins worked behind the others, giggling as they picked up small branches and put them into piles. Piplee was a five-year-old boy, with big, round black eyes and black hair and looked like his father. His three-year-old sister Chae had her Cambodian mother's long face, small black eyes, and black hair. Wong worked along with them and kept an eye on them.

Every day at noon, everyone stopped working and returned home for lunch. Moy's uncle's house was about forty feet in front of Moy's. His house was built with boards he had brought from Pailin. The house was about six feet high, grass roofed like all the rest, and not much bigger than a king-sized bed. Almost all the space in the house was taken up by the bed, where the whole family ate and slept. It was on a board platform, about five inches above the ground. Their cooking stove was outside with a roof but close to the house.

Moy's house was different. It was nine or ten feet high and built of tree trunks; the bed was three feet above the floor and against the back wall. The whole house was about twelve feet wide and fifteen feet long. Moy and Keem tied a big sheet of blue, white, and green plastic to the inside walls, keeping out the wind and rain. The stove was a foot from the front wall and about two feet from the bed. In front of the house was a tall tree. And beneath it was a section of a large block of wood about two feet high, which they used as a table, with three smaller tree sections as chairs. Inside the house were a similar "table" and "chairs." They ate outside in good weather and inside when it rained. It was hard for everyone to get used to the new home and furniture, but they knew life must go on.

On their new bed, Moy and Keem slept on the left, Grandpa on the right. They kept their belongings in between. One night, as they lay in bed, Keem asked Wong, "Dad, what we grow on our land?"

"We grow what people grow," Wong answered in a sleepy voice. "Square stomach grow corn, beans, and tree potato. Tree potato—Yucca not useful; they turn black if they out of ground too long. Then they no good to eat."

"Grandpa, why they no good to eat?" Moy wanted to know.

"They taste bitter." Wong sounded wide awake now. "It best we grow more corn and sweet potato; they keep longer. But we can grow tree potato around edge of our private land. More we grow, more food we have to eat."

"But where we find seed?" Moy asked.

"Open your eye big, big and see," Wong said.

"I see square stomach take rice to town, exchange for potato root, tree potato branch, and corn seed," Keem put in. "Tomorrow, Moy and I go to town and see if we can swap rice for root and seed. More corn, that good!"

"Why?" Moy asked.

"Don't ask too much! Wait and see and learn!" Keem spoke sharply to her daughter.

Wait and see, wait and learn. What can I see or learn inside a jungle like this? Moy wondered. Her thoughts went around and around, but no answer came. Finally, she drifted off to sleep.

The next morning, Moy was awakened by her mother around five o'clock. She washed her face as she was told. Within five minutes, they were both on their way to town on the small brown dirt road that led them to the east, where the town was. To their left, more houses were being built, but to the right, there were only trees and tall grasses. They talked and laughed all the way to town. Once in a while, they passed Chinese or Khmer groups, who were also laughing and talking.

Moy and Keem had rice tied inside their shawls and carried them over their shoulders. After they had walked about an hour and a half, they were close to town. About a twenty-minute walk north from the main road was the house of an old Khmer farmer, who still lived there. Mother and daughter walked to the house, met the Khmer family, and exchanged five or six cans of rice for the tree potato branches, sweet potato roots, and corn seeds. They tied the roots and branches into big bundles and carried them over their shoulders with a carry stick. The roots were heavy, but Moy didn't complain. She knew her mother's burden was even heavier, since Keem carried the tree potato branches and about ten or fifteen cans of corn seeds. They stopped to rest when things got too heavy. But they didn't have to throw anything away. Their necks and backs were bent and stiff from the heavy load. It took them more than three hours to get home. It was very late. They just ate dinner, took baths, and went to bed.

11

When the sun was born in the sky the next morning, Moy, Keem, and Wong were already digging holes with shovels, knives, and sticks on their half of the private land they shared with Moy's third uncle. They planted tree potatoes to the left of the house. In the back, they planted beans near the house and corn behind the beans. The sweet potatoes they grew on the right, in a section they shared with Moy's uncle, who had more land.

For several days, they worked on their private land from dawn to dusk. But after that, Moy and her mother and everyone else had to work on both the common and their private land. The work was hard, and there was a shortage of food. But both the old and young men and women worked to cut down trees and burn them each day to get more land for crops. Every day, food supplies were getting lower and lower. The Khmer Rouge no longer gave them rice and salt but told people, "You find your own food."

While they waited for the crops to mature, Moy's family and everyone else ate whatever food they could find, despite the risks. Women and children went into the dense forest to find tree leaves they hoped weren't poisonous. They would boil a handful of rice in a big pot of water. When the rice was done, they would add the leaves and some salt to make a thin, bitter soup. Other times, Moy's family went with others into the banana grove and cut down the green, thumb-sized bananas. They cut them into small pieces and added them to the rice in the soup. When all the little green bananas were gone, they cut down the banana trees and hacked away at the trunks until they could get to the softer pink "white heart." They cut them up like onion wings and put them in the pot with a little salt to cook for lunch and dinner.

The banana soup wasn't poisonous. But the leaf soup made many people very sick. People's stomachs would grow larger and larger from eating the leaf soup, though they had no pain in any part of their bodies. In spite of their swollen stomachs, they were always hungry. If people didn't eat, they would die from hunger. Some people got so sick from the leaf soup that they died.

One day, Wong said to his daughter, "Keem, Moy's stomach big, big, but there nothing in it. Take your gold jewelry to exchange for some rice for her to eat. Many people die because of swollen stomach. I look at child, and I pity her. She never say anything, but she very hungry."

"I go exchange for rice tomorrow," Keem whispered softly.

Moy was on her hands and knees, her little bottom pointed skyward and her cheek nearly on the ground as she blew into the dying fire in the ground stove; her eyes were watering from the thick black smoke. Finally, when her small face was bright red, the fire came to life. She heard the exchange between Keem and Wong, but she didn't say anything. It was true she was hungry. But there was nothing she could do about it. She could not ask her mother to take the gold to the old farmer and exchange it for rice. She knew how much her mother loved gold jewelry and how hard she had worked and saved to buy it, before the Khmer Rouge came. But she was happy Keem had agreed to Wong's request, and the tip of her pink tongue ran around her lips at the thought of thick, dry rice with salt.

She knew deep down why he had asked. Grandpa was as hungry as she was, and his stomach was just as swollen. He would be embarrassed to ask it for himself, because he was older and thought he should be able to control himself better. Moy felt sorry for her sick and old grandpa. He had been sick ever since they entered the forest. Every time he went to relieve himself, there would be blood and tissue in the urine, and he had become weaker day by day. He needed all the food he could get, but there wasn't enough. Moy sat on her heels, staring at the fire. It seemed her grandpa was dying like the fire had been, and he needed some help to get his life going again. Like everyone else, he had to fight to go on living. People were using gold jewelry to buy extra food or to exchange for rice. Some were caught by the Khmer Rouge, who took the gold or rice away. Then they had no gold and no rice.

It was hard for everyone, but every family found its own way of dealing with things. One of Moy's jobs was to wash the family's clothes in the river to the west. Each time she went, she would carry two metal buckets on a carry stick over her shoulders. After she washed all the clothes, she would bathe herself and carry the buckets home full of clean water. To keep the water from spilling as she walked, she broke off branches with large leaves, washed them in the river, and put them over the buckets. The water buckets were about a foot wide and fifteen inches deep. They were very heavy when full of water. Besides the two buckets, Moy also had to carry the heavy wet clothes tied in a bundle and hung from the carry stick close to her chest.

She would walk until her shoulders ached and grew too tired, and then she would stop to rest. The trip took hours (maybe five or close to six). There were twenty or more houses close to the river. After she passed them, there would be nothing but trees and tall grass all the way home. Moy heard the cries of small birds and other animals, but she wasn't frightened. One time, the buckets she borrowed from her neighbors were larger than the other buckets. She left early in the morning and didn't get home until the silver moon was lighting the foot-paths for her. In the dark, she heard wolves calling for each other. She was scared and cried, begging Great-Grandma's and Great-Grandpa's spirits to protect her from harm, all the way home. Keem came and met her at the other side of their block.

"Ma!" Moy screamed crying, feeling happy to see her mother.

"My child! Why so late, you just come home?" Keem took over carrying the water and bundles home. "My child these buckets very big, full, and heavy!" Keem had cried. Some water was used for cooking. Some water was used for Keem's and Wong's baths, and they felt guilty. That night in bed, Moy heard Keem tell Wong the buckets were too large and full of water for Moy, but she didn't dare throw any water away. Keem asked why she didn't throw some water away.

"Today hot, you and Grandpa must bathe," Moy told her mother.

It looked as if life would get easier for Moy when she learned from the others there was a well about an hour from her block. This was about an hour or hour and a half shorter than the trip to the river. She and her mother followed people to the well. It was a large cement one, and there were about sixty to a hundred people living nearby. Moy found out later that they had worked for the sugar company before the Khmer Rouge came. The Khmer Rouge told them to keep the sugar cane fields and go on growing more sugar cane.

With a closer source of water and the crops growing, thing are looking up, Moy thought. But she was wrong. First, they found out the well water was no good. All the food they cooked with it turned yellow. Then people began to have problems relieving themselves. Moy and Keem had to take turns making the long trips to the river again.

The Khmer Rouge was making changes; they gave each block big pots. They made each block build a big common kitchen, with a grass roof and no walls.

One end was a kitchen, and the rest would be a dining area, but there were no tables or chairs. Four or five people in a block would stay and cook for the whole block of people. After a month or two, the Khmer Rouge gave each block some rice and a tiny amount of fish. At lunch- or dinnertime, the cooks would hit something to make a loud noise, and people in the field would cheer. The workers came with their long hunting knives, axes, or shovels over their shoulders. Everyone waited in line, and the cooks divided the food among them. Adults got two small dippers of dry cooked rice and one small dipper of banana-tree hearts with fish soup. Children got half as much. They all had to bring any other additional food they had to the kitchen and share. They sat on the ground and ate.

People were grateful for the food, and no one said anything. But every lunch- or dinnertime, one or two Khmer Rouge would be there. They had long guns over their shoulders, walking around each family as they ate. People couldn't help wondering what the Khmer Rouge were planning for them. Each person could feel the Black Shirts' eyes on their backs.

Sometimes as she ate, Moy could feel the tip of a gun run across her small back, as Black Shirts walked around her family. She would cock her head and look up at them. They would flash their white teeth. She would show them her yellow teeth. Sometimes they would laugh at her or reach down and pat her head. She didn't like any of it, but there was nothing she could do. Every time it happened, her mother's eyes would grow wide with fear, and Grandpa's face would become hard like stone. But they said nothing.

One day, when they got home, Keem yelled at her, "Why you smile at Black Shirt? You not know death when you see it?"

"She a child. It all right. They smile at her; she smile at them," Wong answered in Moy's defense.

"Black Shirt hate Chinese. They want to eat our flesh!" Keem shouted.

"What you want me do?" Moy asked. "You think I like gun on my back? I don't! If I not look at them, they know I afraid of them. If I let them know I afraid, they keep come back to me. They let me see their white teeth. I let them see my ugly broken yellow teeth, to spoil their appetite so they can't eat rice anymore. Then we have more rice to eat!" Moy smiled sweetly at her mother.

"If it mean that, you better show your teeth often," Wong said through his laughter, as he sat on his side of the bed. Keem sat with her back to the wall. And Moy lay on the bed, using her mother's lap as a pillow. They continued to speak softly for a while. And Moy fell asleep.

A few days later, there was a block meeting. The headman told everyone, "Tomorrow, everyone must go work and eat in town." If they liked, they could sleep there too. About four the next morning, the group from the block went to town together. Ten minutes outside the main town, the Khmer Rouge met with everyone in an open field. Afterward, the Black Shirts gave shovels, hoes, and wheelbarrows to each headman, who distributed them to the men, women, and children in his block. Everyone began to work. Some places were easy to dig, but others were hard, because of rocks and tree roots. By noon, thousands of people, each in their own block group, waited in a big circle for the Khmer Rouge to give them food. The work was hard, but the food was good—thick dry rice and meat cooked with vegetables. Moy and Keem saved some of their food for Grandpa at home.

This went on for a month or two. But no one had any idea why they were digging and shoveling. Later, they learned they were digging ditches that would be part of an irrigation system. Some families slept together in groups near the field. People were pretty happy because the food was good. Then the real nightmare began. The Khmer Rouge began to separate people into different groups by age and sex: children nine to thirteen, adolescents fourteen to eighteen, young people nineteen to twenty-five, women and men over twenty-five. Families could eat lunch and dinner together and sleep together at night. But anyone who wanted to see his or her family at any other time had to ask the leader's permission. That didn't seem so bad at first, but it turned out bad for the children.

Adults could get together at night and go home or sleep near the field. But children old enough to work were forbidden to leave the group they were in. Some parents took food with them and went to eat lunch with their children. But the children couldn't leave the place where their group was located. The Khmer Rouge themselves were the children's group leaders—a man for the boys and a woman for the girls. Children slept with their group near the fields at night, some on the ground and others in hammocks. Moy was with the children, but she didn't stay there long.

12

Moy worked with the children two days and slept with them one night. During those two days, Keem came to eat lunch and dinner with her and talked to her with tears rolling down her cheeks. The second afternoon, Moy could stand it no longer. She asked her leader's permission to go see her mother.

"Buddy Big Sister, I want go see my mother," Moy said in a small voice, in Khmer. Her leader's face was hard and full of hatred. Her leader was a big woman of eighteen or nineteen, a Khmer Rouge, with a square face, dark skin, and black hair that hung a bit below her ears. She wore the standard black sarong and shirt, black tire sandals, and plaid shawl. She asked in a hard tone, "Why buddy want go meet mother?"

"I miss my mother." Moy looked down at her dirty bare feet.

"Miss mother! Buddy, you just see your mother at lunch. Now you want go meet mother again?" The leader spoke sharply, but Moy continued to stare at her feet. "Look at other buddy. They younger than buddy, but they break ties with their father and mother." The other children began to join in with the leader's laughter. "And they not go see father and mother. Buddy, you miss nurse your mother's breast?" The leader and the other children laughed louder at Moy. She could feel her cheeks get hot and tears fill her eyes.

Moy didn't say anything. She turned away, picked up the closest shovel she could find, and started to dig quickly and angrily. That only made the other children laugh more loudly, but Moy didn't care. *If that whore thinks I'm going to stay another day with her...* Moy was too angry to think of a worse name for her leader. And she continued to dig with the shovel, as if she could dig that woman's brain out.

That night after dinner, Moy told her leader she needed to go to the outhouse. The leader looked at her with hatred but told her to go and hurry back.

Moy did hurry back—but not to the group. She hurried home, home, sweet home where her mother and grandfather were. It took about ten minutes to walk to the banana grove with the adults who were heading home and another twenty minutes get to the small footpath leading to her house. She was the only child among the adults. Some of them looked at her and said, "She run away."

Moy heard one woman say, "My child very scared of Khmer Red and do what they tell them. They scared to run home. But she not scared." The farther she walked, the thinner the group got, and finally Moy was all alone on the footpath.

The bright moon was the child's lantern to light her way home. The sweet wind blew gently to keep her company. The soft sound of the doves comforted her, reminding her she was going home, where love was waiting for her. The grass was still wet from the rain and cleaned her dirty feet as she walked on it.

When Moy was in front of the rows of sweet potatoes, she called out in Chinese. Her throat was tight, and tears were falling from her cheeks. "Ma! Grandpa! I come home!"

"Moy? Moy!" she heard them shout. Keem was out of the house in a second to greet her. Happy tears fell from both the mother's and daughter's eyes. Keem was on her knees hugging her daughter. Both were crying and shaking with happiness. Then she got up slowly and led Moy by the hand into the house.

"You come home!" Wong greeted his granddaughter in a broken voice.

"Grandpa!" Moy went to stand between his legs and hug him as he sat on the bed. Her wet cheek nestled against his soft belly. His strong arms hugged her tight, and Moy felt safe. She could feel his cheek resting on her small head.

"You run home?" Wong asked.

Moy drew back her head and saw the most beautiful smile on her beloved grandpa's face. "Yes. I tell Black Shirt I go shit. But I run home instead!" Moy smiled sweetly at him and slowly closed her eyes. She put her cheek back on his belly and sighed happily as she hugged him tighter. She heard a soft voice that seemed far, far away, "She...asleep."

The next thing Moy heard was soft whispering, and slowly, she opened her eyes, not knowing where she was at first. She turned onto her stomach and pushed her head out from the small mosquito net that covered the bed. She saw her mother standing in the doorway, as if she was about to leave. She turned to look at Grandpa, who was sitting on the edge of his side of the bed, smiling at her. She smiled back and called sleepily, "Ma...?"

"Little puppy wake up," Grandpa teased.

Keem turned at the sound of her daughter's voice and smiled at the sleepy face peering out through the mosquito net. Keem walked over, patted her head, and whispered, "I tell your grandpa not to let you go back. I scare, if you go back, next time Black Shirt not let you come see me again. I go work and bring rice for you to eat. Don't leave house! Stay inside. Go back to sleep. I go work now." Keem smiled at Moy and then turned to look at her father and remind him one last time, "Don't let her out!" She turned on her heel and was gone.

Moy turned to look at her Grandpa, rubbing her eyes with the back of her hand. "Grandpa, what time is it?"

"Four thirty."

"Four thirty?" Moy's eyes were as wide as an owl's.

Wong laughed softly and teased, "Little puppy hug me till she fall asleep."

Moy looked at her grandfather shyly. He had no shirt on, just a pair of light-blue shorts, and sat cross-legged on the bed. *He looks like a handsome angel!* she thought sadly. She studied him closely. His face was getting longer and had very few wrinkles. Even with the hard life they had had, he still looked younger than his age, which he told her was sixty-one. His high cheekbones were more promi-nent now that he was getting thinner. He had a perfect nose, not too large and not too small, just beautiful. And his lips were wide and thin. No wonder women had been crazy about him when he was younger. Even when they were in Pailin, some shameless Chinese and Khmer women had turned around and looked at him as he walked by.

"What you look at?" Wong asked with a smile.

"You." Moy turned away, smiling too.

"What about me?"

"Tell me about the woman who send you their pictures when you return to China from Thailand?"

"I tell you hundred time. You not bored?"

"I not bored. Tell!"

"Your great-grandma send me to my father's house in Thailand. I the young-est boy in family. My mother not want her youngest son go fight Japanese. I teenager then, and I want go chase Japanese out of China. But she won't let me. I go to Thailand help your great-grandpa and my older brother with tofu busi-ness. I stay there five or six years. I twenty-three when I go back to China." Wong paused, shaking his head slowly, laughing softly to himself, as if overwhelmed with joy at his memories.

"I over twenty and my ma call me 'child.' She hug me and cry, 'Child, child!' Everyone in train station stop to look at us, you know. Chinese parent not usually do that in public." Wong laughed louder and seemed to become that young man in his mother's arms again—so happy and carefree and just a bit embarrassed.

Moy smiled too, feeling happy for him. She knew the story by heart, having listened to it a hundred times, but she loved to hear it from him. *If this is how I can make him forget what's happening now, I'll do everything in my power to get him to tell me about his youth again and again,* Moy thought.

She put her chin on her palms and turned to look at him as he continued. "When I get home, my ma take out two hundred picture of so many girl, who live in our village and some from other village. They think I rich! I laugh and laugh when I see those picture. But your great-grandma make me sit down and look through them. Some girl fat like mother pig. Some thin like stick. I like only one girl of two hundred picture; she beautiful. I marry her within five month. I stay in China till Keem year and half and your big uncle four months old. Then I go to Cambodia.

"I not speak Khmer or understand Khmer. I go kill pig for living. I gamble too. I like gambling…I win lot of money. The casino owner's daughter follow me around. She know I very poor, but she not care. She very beautiful. I tell her I have two child. And she say, 'I love them as my own child. But I want to be with you and be your small wife.' When I not take her, she still not angry with me. But she keep follow me around, and every time I gamble, I always win. Then I realize. She tell her father let me win, no matter what, in hope I take her as second wife. Her father like me too. He always ask me eat with him…give me good food and wine. That help because I not have much money. I save all money I make from gambling and killing pig and send it to your grandma in China.

"I kill pig and gamble for ten year. Then one day, I send all money to your grandma to come to Cambodia with your mother and big uncle." Wong's voice always became bitter when he came to this part.

Moy didn't want to see him hurt, so she interrupted him. "Grandpa, go to sleep now."

But he didn't listen to her and went on with the story, his deep voice sounding angry. "I go to airport wait for them. I very happy wait to see them again. When my old woman come out of plane, I see only your big uncle, but no Keem. I ask her where Keem? And she say, 'Keem in China with her grandma.' I very angry with her. I lose control and slap her. And I never see my daughter again till she eighteen year old.

"Eight year later, I go back to China. I wait for them in train station. I see a woman who look about fifty. I walk past her few time. Each time I pass, she look at me in strange way but never say a word." Wong stopped for a few minutes, as if it was too painful to go on.

Moy wished she had kept her big mouth shut! Her small face was as hard as her grandfather's as she shared his pain.

Wong's voice was like stone when he continued, "I think to myself, *What a shameless woman! She keep look at me like she never see a man before. Ugly woman, face and hands all wrinkle! Shameless woman!* Then I see your great-grandma come run to me. She hug me and call me, 'Child, child!' She cry so hard and can't talk for long time.

"And this ugly woman keep look at me, then she start to cry too. Then she come up to me and call me, 'Dad.' My eighteen-year-old daughter look like fifty-year-old woman! If your great-grandma not there to tell me that ugly woman is my daughter, I think the woman crazy. I not know what to say to her. I just stand there and look at my daughter, who look older than me. Tear roll from my eyes and the first word I say, 'My sad child.'

"When we get home, Keem ask if I come to take her to Cambodia with me. I say no. But I feel very sad for my daughter. And I promise her that I send for her after I return to Cambodia. I work hard and save every penny and send it to her. My heart break when I get on train back to Hong Kong. Keem run after train and cry, 'Dad, don't run away from me!' I cry too, and I not feel embarrass.

"When I get back to Cambodia, I work harder than ever. I not spend any money. I think only about my daughter, who still live in China and work hard on government farm. After many year, I send all the money I save to your great-grandma to come to Cambodia with Keem. But your great-grandma send me letter, say she not want to come. But she send Keem to me.

"Keem twenty-seven when she come to Cambodia. Everything new to her. She never see car before. She's like a little girl, so happy to see everything. She happy at first, to meet her five brother and three sister and her mother. If she work hard in China, she work even harder in Cambodia. She the oldest, she have to take care of eight brother and sister. She cook and clean for them, but they not like her. And they look down on her.

"I not know what happen at home. I out of house before sunrise and come home after sunset. I not see Keem or rest of family much. Then one day, two year later, I come home from work, Keem gone. My old woman tell me, 'Keem not happy.' I ask her why, she just say, 'Keem not happy.' I not know where Keem go. I worry to death because everything still new to her, and she not speak Khmer. I like crazy man, go look for Keem three or four month. I never go home. I go everywhere in Phnom Penh look for her. But I never find my daughter. Then I give up and go home, and my old woman give me letter from Keem. Keem marry a Chinese man, who live in same town with us in China. They go live in Siem Reap. I very happy my sad daughter safe and have a husband. But I still want to know why she run away from home." Wong paused, turned to look at Moy, and asked, "You know why she run away? Your ma tell you why?"

"Yes, she tell." Moy felt as if she wanted to shout out her mother's pain. She remembered only too well why her mother had run away from home. But Moy didn't call it home. She called it a hell cell, a freedom cage.

13

Moy remembered every word of her beloved mother's life story. She had listened to it just as often as she had listened to Grandpa's tales. Keem had never had an easy life, even as a young girl.

"When I first come to Cambodia, everything new to me. Even cooking stove. In China, Great-Grandma is poor; we not have money to buy wood to make fire. Every day, I go to mountain to pick up leaf and dry them in the sun and make fire to cook food. We need lot of leaf to cook one meal. When I older, I work in rice field and salt mine for government. Once a week, I get my share of food from government. If I work seven day, I get more food. Each day I sick, they cut one day food off. I share my food, rice and meat, with Great-Grandma. After work, I go to mountain to get leaf for fire.

"I like work. Great-Grandma love me very much. Every time she look at my two hand, she cry, 'Sad child!' because salt eat all my skin nearly to bone. I work hard every day to get enough food for us. Then one day, Great-Grandma say, 'Your father send money for you go to him.' I very happy, but I feel sad Great-Grandma not want to go with me. I go to Hong Kong. I buy new clothe, shoe, and sunglass for me!"

Moy still had her ma's sunglasses.

"I buy new clothe, shoe, and food and send them to Great-Grandma in China. I stay in Hong Kong one week, then I go meet my father. Dad tell me when he come to China, I have five brother and three sister; in Cambodia, I meet them all. Mother and the rest very friendly to me, but only for few hour. Then they call me stupid because I not know anything. I never use wood to make fire before. We have big kitchen, big tall sink, and if I want water, I just turn that metal handle and water come. But I not know how to turn it on and off! Everyone laugh at me and say, 'You very stupid! You not know anything!'

"I learn fast, but it make no difference. I wash their clothes, and it hurt my hand, where salt eat the skin away. And my hand stay in soap water hour after hour wash the clothes. After that, I cook and clean. But I never please them. Your grandma yell at me that clothes not clean and make me wash them again. When clothes tear, she say, 'You too clean, wash clothes too hard. That why they tear so easy. It yours fault!' Then she pull my hair and hit me. No one help me. They laugh at me. She never let me go outside, just stay home and work. Your youngest aunt, she my mother's favorite. I worse than a slave to your grandma. But my youngest brother love me. But he too little, seven or nine year old, not understand anything. One time, he ask me, 'Big Sister, why Mother hit you?' I tell him, I not know why. He cry with me and tell me, 'Big Sister, I love you.' I love him very much.

"I get up early to cook their morning meal. Then wash their clothes till lunchtime. After I cook lunch, I take care of your youngest aunt while other eat. Sometimes they eat everything. And I have nothing to eat all day. They have full belly and time to play. I work all day and eat nothing. Then I can take it no longer, all the beating and yelling from your grandma and laughter from all my brother and sister. But my youngest brother not laugh like other, he cry. And Mother hate him! She yell at him, 'Bad son! Short life!' He cry in my arm; we cry together. One night, after I live there nearly two year, I run away. I go to the Mekong River that run from Phnom Penh to China. I want it take me back to China, to Great-Grandma. I cry, feel very sad. I nearly jump in the river. But someone stop me.

"This person hold me tight to keep me from jump in the river. He ask why I want to kill myself. When I turn to look at him, I recognize him. His name is Luck. He make me sit down. Tell him why I come to Cambodia. And why I run away? And why I want to kill myself? After I tell him what happen. He take me to his mother's home. I stay there for a while. He promise not to tell my mother that I live with his mother. We like each other, and we marry few month later. Then we go live in Siem Reap.

"Then I write letter and sent it to your grandpa. He come to see us. And I tell him everything. I ask him not to beat my mother when he return home. He say he won't. But he very angry with 'the old woman.' He leave few day later, go back to Phnom Penh.

"We not have money. We eat boil pig's skin in soy sauce and rice, every day. Luck and I sell vegetable seed for living. Luck go to Phnom Penh many time to buy vegetable seed and bring them home, so we can sell them. Then one day, Luck not come home. I wait and wait, but he never come. By then, I have you for five month, still inside my belly. I not know what to do. I have little money, and I not want to lose you. I write letter to your grandpa. And he come two day later.

"Grandpa stay with me and help to feed me. He want me to stay home. But I not listen to him. I carry steamed fish to sell from street to street. He very angry. But I tell him, what I do make baby strong. He not say much after that. But he not happy with what I do. I keep carry fish and sell, till you eight month in me, and business very good! When people see my big belly, they feel sorry for me and buy more fish than they need.

"When you five month old, Luck come home. He buy two tiny dress for you. He take you to picture booth and take your picture. You too little to sit. He pull your dress back from behind chair, to hold you up. He stay few day. Then he want to take us to Phnom Penh with him. But I not want to go. He threaten to take you from me. But Grandpa there to help.

"Grandpa say no one take his granddaughter away from him, without fight. Only fool want to fight your grandpa. He very good with Chinese kung fu. He almost have black belt. Great-Grandma tell me when he thirteen, he fight three big boy. And each boy have broken face, arm, and leg. Your great-grandpa and old uncle teach him, when he small boy. After your grandpa's threat, Luck leave us alone. He go to Phnom Penh and never come back again.

"When you three year old, Luck's mother send me letter say he get sick and die. I not cry for him. But I cry for you. You not know what your father look like and not have father to take care of you and play with you like other child. But you always happy with me and Grandpa. And he love you very much, and I love you too."

Although, Keem had suffered under her cruel mother's hands and abuses every day, she still sent money once or twice a year to her mother in Phnom Penh. Moy remembered Grandpa gave his wife money and told her, "Keem send them for you." She smiled and couldn't stop saying good things about Keem. And Grandpa said, "Remember what you just say, when you spend all Keem's money. But I know you, when Keem's money gone, you go back and say bad thing about Keem again."

If I was Ma, I wouldn't give her mother a penny! But Ma has a good heart, filled with pure love and as giving as Buddha, and as bright as the sun. And that is a fact. Moy remembered a couple of times, Keem gave her five thousand nings to take to her mother. Keem's mother lived with her two younger sisters and the fourth brother, about an hour away from them, in Pailin. Moy asked her mother why she gave Grandma so much money.

"Child look after and feed their mother and father."

"Grandma never good to you."

"Good or bad, she my mother. I have to respect her and feed her."

Moy did bring the money to Grandma. But she didn't give her all of it. Moy gave her grandma only a thousand or two thousand and brought the rest back. She gave the money to her mother and told Keem and Wong Grandma was too old to count so much money. Besides, she loved Grandma. She would get to see Grandma more often, if Ma gave a hundred ning at a time. That way, Grandma would have more nice things to say about her mother. "Grandma count how often you send her money, not how much. I say fifty ning still too much!" Moy remembered Wong had laughed at her and Keem had shaken her head. "You think I not know? You bring money to Grandma behind my back?" Moy told her mother.

Keem screamed and made a grab for her. "You!"

"Don't fool around with her. She know everything!" Wong shouted with laughter.

14

And yes, that was a fact. They both love me more than anything on this earth. If I asked for the moon, they would give it to me, if they could, Moy thought. She had always been completely happy with them, and they had always treasured her—*except for that one time.* Comparing her life to her mother's, it was like sky and earth. Moy had everything; Keem had had nothing. Even now, Moy still had everything she needed. Life was hard. But she still had her mother's and grandpa's love, and that was all she needed. Their warm love filled the emptiness in her belly. And she could still see the rest of her family. Here in the forest, it was good to see those unloving uncles and aunts once in a while.

The only uncle Moy wanted to see was her youngest uncle, but he died when he was very young, between fifteen and seventeen years old. They were like big brother and little sister. They loved each other. They played and went everywhere together. He came to live with his beloved big sister Keem after Moy was born. Moy remembered she cried when he was killed. Her young uncle had had a fight with his fourth brother, who wanted the watch that Grandpa and Ma had brought for him. Her young uncle got beaten up by his older, mean, and greedy brother. He took off for Vietnam, joined the army, and got himself killed.

About seven or eight months after they came to the forest, the Khmer Rouge agreed to take all the Vietnamese back to Vietnam. Moy's oldest uncle's wife spoke some Vietnamese, and her family went to Vietnam. Everyone else in the family followed her, except Moy, Keem, and Wong. Wong warned his children not to be fooled by the Khmer Rouge's words. How could they believe the Black Shirts, who had forced them out of their hometown, were now being kind to them? But no on listened to him. They were the only three in the family who stayed behind.

They had been in the forest for about a year and the corn and potatoes were just fully grown when they were forced to move again, leaving the crops behind. Once again, everyone had to move all their belongings to an unknown town, about an hour and a half away. Wong had already gone ahead to the new town. During the move, an unusual thing happened. One afternoon during the last week of the move, Moy and her mother were having lunch inside Keem's brother's house, where they lived after he went to Vietnam. They heard someone calling from outside. Moy went out to look and saw a dark, handsome young man with high cheekbones and a small, round chin; he was about five feet eight or nine inches tall. He was dressed in black like the Khmer Rouge, but he had no gun. He showed his white, beautiful teeth and spoke in a deep voice, "Hello, Buddy Little Sister. Can I have some water to drink?"

"Yes!" Moy nearly ran for her life. *Black Shirts should be in the new town, not here. Maybe he came to kill us, or worse!* Moy thought; she was frightened. She didn't dare stop to think about that but ran breathlessly to tell her mother. "Ma! It Black Shirt out there, and he ask for water."

"I no Black Shirt," he spoke up behind her, in broken Chinese, in the Chau Chow dialect. He laughed when Moy nearly jumped out of her pants. "I know you scare, when you look at me with white face and eye big, big. I dress like Black Shirt. But people in sugar cane field must all wear black." He stopped when he saw Moy and Keem staring at him with their mouths open.

Keem recovered first. "You look like Black Shirt. Your skin dark like them. If you not speak Chau Chow, I say you Black Shirt." They both laughed. But Moy went to hide behind the bed and wished the earth would open up and swallow her. She was too embarrassed to face him again. "My daughter very shy," Keem told the young man.

"I scare her out there," he told Keem. Then he shouted to Moy in Khmer, "Buddy Little Sister! Big brother beg forgiveness for scare you!"

Moy wished he hadn't shouted. She felt her cheeks get even hotter. She wished he would go away fast. But he didn't. Even worse, her mother asked him to have lunch with them. Moy had no choice but to join them. While they ate, the young man told them his parents were Vietnamese. They had died when he was a small boy, and he had gone to live with an aunt and uncle. But none of them cared about him. He left them and went to live with someone else. But the new family was no better. They worked him from morning to sunset in the rice field. Sometimes, they gave him only two meals a day. Sometimes, he got none, and he had to go out and beg for food.

Keem and Moy felt sorry for him, whether or not he was telling the truth. He was only eighteen, but he looked much older. His name was Chi Minh. But Keem called him Ming in Chinese. After that, Ming came to eat lunch with Keem and Moy every day. He always brought sugar, rice, and dried fish for them. The Khmer Rouge fed the sugar cane field workers better than the farmers. Ming would always tell them he had wanted a brother and sister when he was a boy. Keem told him if he became her son, he would have a little sister. He agreed without a second thought. Keem told him she didn't want to hear any more "Buddy" business when he was with the family. He should call his new sister by her real name or call her "Moy."

Moy was very happy. She had always wanted a brother or sister herself. But she knew she would never have one. Keem didn't want to marry again. It wasn't like she still loved Luck, but she was afraid. She might marry a man who would abuse Moy. Keem would never want that. Now Moy had a big brother! The two of them got along better than Keem could have hoped for. Ming called Keem "Ma" just like Moy. Keem was very happy to have this new son, because he made Moy happy, and it was good for Moy to have a big brother, who adored her and took care of her. Keem told her father about Ming. Wong was happy to have a new grandson and couldn't wait to meet him. Keem told Wong Ming had to work and couldn't come to meet him. Wong was very disappointed.

But to their surprise, the next day, Ming came early in the morning and offered to help Keem and Moy move. Keem kept chasing him back to work, worried the Khmer Rouge might not give him food and might even beat him up. But Ming only laughed at her worries.

"They not beat me, Ma. And they give me food when I return. I tell them I just find my ma and little sister and I want to see them. I ask for two day, come to see you. They let me. Don't worry! They not beat me, and they not kill me either." It was a mistake for him to add those words.

"No! You go back to work for them. I miss you; as long as you safe, I happy. But go back now!" Keem pushed and shoved him out the door.

While he laughed helplessly, Moy was giggling at the worried look on her mother's face. She came to her big brother's defense. "Ma, if Big Brother say it all right, it all right. Let him come to our new home and meet Grandpa."

"You my daughter. You tell your big brother go back right now, if you love him."

"Big Brother, I love you; you come."

"Ooo!" Keem cried in defeat, as Moy and her new brother giggled. "Like brother, like sister." Keem added, worried and unhappy. It was two against one, and Keem gave in. But she could not help but worry about her new son, who was as stubborn as her daughter. Try as she might, she couldn't change his mind.

Ming was certainly a big help. He carried the biggest and heaviest boxes. Keem told him to carry the smaller ones, but he didn't listen. He told her, "You my ma, you must not carry anything. Let's go! I want to meet Grandpa!" Even a fool could see the pride on Keem's face at her new son's behavior. On the way to the new house, Keem wanted to take turns carrying the boxes. But Ming refused, telling her not to worry, asking if she was tired and wanted to stop and rest. Moy carried two smaller boxes and walked behind Ming, struggling to keep up. If he got very far ahead, he would put down his boxes and come back to carry Moy's. Then Keem would pick up the bigger boxes. Ming would drop Moy's boxes and run chasing after his mother to get the larger boxes back.

By this time, the roof on the house was done. But there were no walls and no bed. Wong was very pleased with his new grandson and Ming with his new grandpa. After lunch, Ming wanted to help build the walls, but Wong wouldn't let him, saying the townspeople would do that. They just unpacked their belongings. That night, Moy and Keem slept on the pieces of boards next to the right wall and Grandpa next to the left. Ming slept in his hammock in the middle. He offered the hammock to anyone who wanted it. But no one knew how to sleep in one.

Ming went back to the sugar cane fields the next morning. After he left, Keem told her father she got up four times in the night to cover Ming with his blanket. Each time she got up, she found his blanket on the floor. And she couldn't sleep worrying that he might catch a cold in the chilly night air. Three weeks later, Ming returned to see them again. By this time, the house had walls and a bed. That afternoon, Keem cooked rice and a small chicken. She put the food on the mat and told Moy and Ming to go outside and pray to the sky and the earth. Moy and Ming did this. They swore and became "big brother and little sister for life." Ming asked Keem if he could take his little sister with him. The Khmer Rouge fed them better in the sugar cane fields. He didn't want his new sister to go hungry. Keem and Wong let Moy go with their blessing. Moy and Ming left that afternoon for the sugar cane field.

At the sugar cane fields, all the houses were built with boards and had metal-covered roofs, like the houses in Pailin. The common kitchen was big, and there were several long tables that seated about forty people each. Every worker wore black clothes and black tire-tread sandals with different colors of plaid shawls around their necks.

Moy felt her cheeks get hot, because she was dressed differently from everyone else. She wore long yellow pants with red flowers and a pink short-sleeved shirt with small flowers, and her feet were bare. She wished she had never come here. Ming sensed her discomfort and bent down to talk to her in Khmer, in a comforting voice. "Don't feel uncomfortable. They good people. You can make friend with them. You not have to eat with children or old people. You eat with me until you feel comfortable. Then go eat with children. Here, children eat first, then old people. I eat whenever I want, because I drive tractor. Khmer Red treat tractor driver special. You hungry now?"

"I want to eat with Big Brother," Moy told him shyly, looking down at her dirty bare feet.

Ming sat on his heels and pushed her chin up with his thumb; he looked into her eyes and spoke in Khmer. "Don't look down when you talk to me or anyone else. Stand up straight. And don't let any of them look down on you. You as good and as important as any of them. Don't let your shyness make you put yourself down. If you let them, they look down on you. Understand?" Moy nodded, fighting back tears. His big hand came down on her head, and he led her to his friends.

All Ming's friends were men and all Khmers. Everyone was very friendly to Moy.

"Ming, who she?" one friend asked.

"My little sister. She come here to live with me," he told his friend proudly, smiling down at Moy.

"She pretty," put in another friend. Moy looked away shyly.

"My little sister very shy. Don't tease her." Ming tipped his sister's head back and smiled handsomely down at her. She couldn't help but smile back.

"She more pretty when she smile," a smaller man said as he came toward the group. All the men laughed and teased when they saw Moy's face get red as fire.

"My little sister pretty, and you too old!" Ming snapped at the smaller man, and the rest laughed louder. "You like embarrass woman, Buddy Brother. But I not let you embarrass my little sister," Ming told his friend, teasing but angry at the same time.

"Be careful and stay away from his little sister, or he eat your head off!" An older man put in. But the smaller man didn't seem to notice the threat. He came and stood next to Ming and put his arm around his shoulder.

"This rude one is my good buddy," Ming told his sister. Ming's friend was about a head shorter and much smaller than Ming. His face was long, with high cheekbones and small black eyes. *He looks as if he just got up from a sickbed,* Moy thought. His skin was much paler than her brother's. The two of them stood together; one looked like a dark, handsome angel, and the other…

"Let's go eat rice," the smaller man said, smiling down at Moy. The men laughed louder, when they saw Ming pull his friend to the other side of him. Ming walked between his friend and Moy. But Ming's friend was in a playful mood. Once in a while, he changed sides and walked next to Moy. When that happened, Ming would take his sister by the shoulder and pull her to the other side. And the men would laugh again.

About twenty-five or thirty of Ming's fellow workers were having dinner at a long table. Moy sat next to her brother and ate the thick, dry rice and big pieces of meat cooked with vegetables. She wasn't afraid when one of the Khmer Rouge came up and asked who she was. Before she could answer, Ming told him who she was and why she was there. The Black Shirt didn't say anything. He smiled warmly, sat down next to her, and had dinner with them. Moy wasn't afraid, because Ming was there to protect her. She knew there wasn't much he could do, but somehow, she felt safer.

After dinner, Moy met a tiny woman no taller than her own four feet but much fatter. Her name was Chin. She had a round face, small black eyes, very white skin, and short hair like a man's. She had a sweet smile and was very friendly. She talked to Moy a few minutes and then left. Ming told Moy he wanted to marry that woman, but she had turned him down many times. He wouldn't give up though.

No, he wouldn't give up, Moy thought. She had only known him a few weeks, but she knew he wasn't the type to give up without a fight. *The woman must be a fool to turn him down…she isn't even pretty. And he is strong, handsome, caring, kind, and understanding.* In just the short time Moy had spent in her brother's company, she saw so many women follow him around, wanting his attention. When they were unsuccessful, they would take Moy's hand and talk to her very kindly. Ming was pleased, but only in a friendly way.

That night, Ming took Moy to Chin's stepmother's house to spend the night. He told his sister he would see her in the morning and promised he would ask the Khmer Red for new clothes and shoes for her. Moy was too scared to sleep at first. When she did fall asleep, she had a nightmare. Her mother was bitten by a snake and died. She woke up, got out of bed, and tiptoed out of the house.

Outside, she knelt down and prayed over and over, "Great-Grandma, Great-Grandpa, don't let anything happen to Ma. Look after her. Safe her and I cook rice and chicken and pray to you." Then she was on her way home before the sun was born for the new day.

15

It was dark, but she could see where she was going. Moy was the only living soul on the small footpath leading home. On both sides were trees, grass, birds, wolves, and other animals crying in the forest. She wasn't afraid of them. But she was afraid for her mother's life and couldn't wait to get home to her. The longer she walked, the brighter the sky got.

Moy entered the new town from the back, at the first line of the houses. She saw her mother doing something in front of the house. Moy was very happy to see her mother safe. She shouted, "Ma! Ma!" She saw her mother turn around. She looked surprised.

"Moy?"

"Ma! I come home!" Moy shouted happily, running to hug her mother hard around the waist.

"Where your big brother?" Keem demanded, hugging her daughter.

"Big brother in sugarcane field. I come alone because I dream snake bite you and you die. I pray to Great-Grandma and Great-Grandpa; I cook rice and chicken and pray to them if nothing happen to you." Moy closed her eyes and breathed in the good smell of her mother's warm body. She felt safe in her mother's arms again.

Keem lifted her daughter's head up and looked into her eyes. "A snake nearly bite me this morning!" Keem told Moy. Moy felt cold sweat running down her back at these words. Keem went on, "I see its tail. I step back fast and scream. Our neighbor Seng come and kill it. He tell me it poisonous snake. One bite and I die in a minute." Keem told her daughter. Moy hugged her mother harder. "Your pray good, but don't make foolish promise when you pray. If we not have rice and chicken, things become worse. Don't fool around when you pray again, hear me?" Moy didn't answer but nodded against her mother's stomach.

"I hear puppy's voice. She run home again?" Moy heard her Grandpa chuckle softly from inside the house. She smiled but didn't let go of her mother. "It eight o'clock? What time you leave your big brother?" Wong asked from the house.

"Don't know," Moy answered and then went inside the house arm in arm with her mother.

"You not tell your big brother when you leave?" Wong asked. Before Moy could answer, he already knew the answer.

"No."

"You not just run away without tell him!" Wong shouted. "He worry what happen to you."

"Big Brother not worry; he know."

"He not know if you not tell him!"

"Then he come to see us," Moy said, smiling sweetly.

Grandpa shook a finger at her and said, "In future, no one want to help you. If you just run away without tell them first."

"Before, you think Black Shirt let me come home if I tell them where I go?" Moy moved her head a little closer to her grandpa smiling. "Huh?" She blinked her eyes at him.

"This one!" Wong frowned deeply and shook his finger harder at her, disapproving. Nevertheless, he seemed happy to have his loose-tongued granddaughter back.

Later, she overhead him tell her mother that with Moy around, he could never be lonely or bored. Sometimes, she made his blood boil and he wanted to kill her. Other times, she made him laugh or smile. But he didn't know what he was smiling about or laughing about. She brought so much joy to his life. He would miss her even when she was gone for just a few short hours. He missed her loose tongue most of all. The girl spoke her mind but never lied. That was why he loved her so much, which made the other grandchildren jealous. He would do everything in his power to protect his beloved granddaughter from harm.

He also complained to Keem about his new grandson's stubbornness; he was like Moy. The two of them would turn his hair gray overnight. Their headstrongness and loose tongues worried him. But he was proud of them both. Hard work and stubbornness would get them out of hell and into heaven. If only they knew how to use their brains. He had no trouble believing his granddaughter would know how, but Ming? The boy seemed smart, hardworking, and loving, but Wong had known him such a short time. It was hard to tell what to think of

Ming. Young men liked to use their fists more than their brains, as Wong remembered all too well from his own youth. But he was still proud to have Ming as a grandson.

Ming and the smaller friend Moy had met came two days later. Ming acted like any true brother would toward a little sister who didn't obey him. Moy wished she had come home an hour later and not had to face him. His handsome face was dark with anger, and there was murderous rage in his black eyes. There was none of the normal laughter in his face. He was sitting in the brown hammock Grandpa had made out of a rice bag when Moy came in with her mother from work. The minute Ming saw her he started to shout at her in Khmer, since his Chinese wasn't good enough to express his anger.

"I worry about you, when you run off without tell me one word. If you want to come home, why you not wait till morning and tell me? Then I take you home. Worst, I scare wolf might eat you up. Then I scare you can't find your way home. What I tell Ma and Grandpa, if I lose you? What happen if you kill by animal? You think I can find another little sister like you for Ma and Grandpa?"

"All right! All right! Stop talk. More you talk, more you sound like toothless grandma!" his small friend interrupted.

Moy saw Ming seemed to be fighting for breath after his long, angry speech.

"Big Brother talk like toothless grandma?" Moy couldn't help giggling at the way her brother was gasping and the way he looked at her. Ming narrowed his eyes.

"You!" He spoke in Chau Chow, pointing at her.

"Me what?" Moy asked innocently, pointing at her own chest. They spoke in Chinese out of courtesy to Wong, who understood very little Khmer.

"Hit her, Ming." Both Keem and Wong spoke up at the same time. They were very disappointed in the girl's behavior.

Both brother's and sister's eyes widened in shock. Moy was shocked. Her mother and grandpa had given her brother permission to punish her for not behaving. They had given him the power that belonged to a real older brother. Ming smiled sweetly and made a grab for his sister's arm from where he sat. Moy tried to jump out of reach, but she wasn't fast enough. She pushed his hand away, screaming with laughter. He let go, lost his balance, and fell backward out of his the hammock, head down and feet up. Keem and Wong screamed in horror, but his friend and his sister screamed with laughter. Ming didn't move for a minute. Keem was beside him, asking if he had been hurt. He said something

Moy couldn't hear, because she was laughing so hard she had tears running down her face.

"Little Sister, help me?" Ming stretched one hand toward her.

Moy shook her head, laughing helplessly with both arms wrapped around her stomach. One minute he was on the ground, and the next he was next to her. He had one hand on her arm, his free hand threatening to come down hard on her bottom. Still laughing, Moy turned left and right to avoid the threatening hand. But he kept following her. Both ended up laughing and giggling until the tears ran from their eyes, and they both received frowns of disapproval from their mother and grandfather.

"I tell you to hit her, not play with her," Wong snapped at his grandson. But somehow, he looked pleased with Ming.

"You spoil her. If you play with her and not hit her," his mother told him.

"I love my little sister. I can't hit her. She too big," Ming said through his laughter, still threatening to spank her with his big palm. "I hit her if she do that again," he announced to everyone. He released his sister's arm and pulled her around to stand in front of him. He looked at her and spoke in Khmer, "You a girl. And girl not walk alone in forest. Many crazy people out there and Khmer Red. If they see you alone, they might rape you. They have gun, and you don't. If people see Khmer Red rape you, they can't help you. And lot of wolf and other animal in forest can kill you. If Khmer Red let me, I come after you same day. But they not let me come. They tell me you run home. Everyone say the same and not worry about you. But I worry. My little sister might get hurt on way home. I know you smart. But I not want you hurt. Don't do anything make me worry about you like that again, hear me?"

Moy felt like crying and wanted to hug him at the same time. But she couldn't. Sisters and brothers at their age didn't hug each other. She just nodded.

"You make good father to some child," Ming's friend teased him, speaking for the first time after a long silence.

Ming turned to his friend and teased back. "I make good father for you too." Everyone laughed.

Moy looked at her ma and grandpa. There was something in their eyes she couldn't define. Love? Hurt? Understanding? Pride? Probably love...but...?

Well, so much anger and so much yelling, but now he wants to take me back with him again, Moy thought, but Keem told Ming to return without his little sister. Moy would likely run home again without telling him if she missed her mother and grandfather. Moy smiled, because her mother knew her all too well.

Ming and his friend went home without Moy. Ming returned whenever the Khmer Rouge let him. Sometimes, he came once a month, sometimes three times a month. Sometimes, he brought rice or dry fish, but mostly he brought sugar. Moy was happy to be with her mother and grandfather and see her big brother once in a while. But her happiness wouldn't last long.

16

They had lived in the new town for three or four months. Some people in town worked on digging the irrigation ditches, and others went to cut down trees on the mountain, clearing the land for farming. Keem stayed home in town and worked on the mountain. Each day, Moy walked the fifteen minutes' distance with Keem, worked beside her mother all day, and returned home with Keem at night. One day, Keem cut her right ankle on the sharp grass. The cut wasn't big or deep, but it somehow got infected and swelled to the size of her finger. The pain made the walking much more difficult, but Keem continued to make the trip to the mountain, saying, "If you not work, you not eat."

Two weeks later, Moy also got a cut on her right ankle. She didn't know how it happened. It was quite small, but it swelled even more than her mother's had. It became the size of a man's thumb. Once Moy got her cut, her mother's cut healed immediately. But that was the only good result of Moy's cut. It hurt her terribly, but she was a fighter. She continued to walk to work on the mountain every day. Everyone was jealous of Keem, because she had her daughter with her, while their children might be hundreds of miles away from them…Buddha knew where. The Khmer Rouge had taken all the children old enough to work away from their families and sent them to work in other places; the parents had no idea where.

One day, the headman came to the house to take Moy away. Wong and Keem protested that Moy couldn't walk because of her ankle. But the headman said he'd let her ride on his bicycle. Moy and Keem cried and hugged each other. But the headman and one of the Khmer Rouge dragged them apart. Moy cried and called for her mother. Her hands stretched out toward Keem, big tears falling from her sad, frightened eyes.

"Ma! Not let them take me!"

The headman dragged Moy from the house, as the Khmer Rouge held on to Keem to keep her from following. Keem kept crying and reaching after Moy, calling her name. Grandpa was too sick and weak to do anything but sit at the edge of the bed watching helplessly and crying.

"Moy! Don't take my only child away from me!" Keem kept screaming over and over, as if she could somehow change their minds.

Moy managed to get free from the headman. She ran with painful steps toward her mother, arms outstretched.

"Ma! I not want to go! Help me!" But the headman followed her into the house and dragged her out again. Blood was all over from her wounded ankle— on the ground and on her clothes. The headman dragged her so roughly she fell hard to the ground. Keem and Wong screamed in horror.

"My child hurt! Don't drag my child!" Keem screamed in terror. "She no dog! My child human like you! But you not human. You not have mercy for human!" Keem kept crying, turning this way and that way in the Khmer Rouge's arms, trying to get free and help her daughter. But the Khmer Rouge was too strong.

Moy screamed with pain as she was dragged away on the ground by the headman, sometimes facedown, sometimes on her side, sometimes on her back. One of her hands was on the ground, trying to grab onto something, scraping the skin from her small palm and leaving a trail of blood behind. The headman didn't stop until he reached the bicycle. Then he pulled her up to her feet so roughly, she nearly fell facedown again. She knocked the bicycle down with her right leg and screamed with new pain as blood gushed from the wound on her ankle.

The headman yanked her roughly closer to him and shouted in her ear, "You want Khmer Red kill your mother and grandpa?" Moy shook her head helplessly, still crying. "Stop cry. Get on bicycle! Or go tell your mother stop argue with Khmer Red, or he kill them!"

Moy pulled away from his grasp and walked as fast as she could to her mother. When she entered the house, the Khmer Rouge was still holding onto her mother's arms. Moy spoke to her mother in Khmer, so as not to anger the Black Shirt.

"Ma, Grandpa, I go now. Don't worry. I be all right." Moy's throat was tight, and she found it hard to breathe. She couldn't have stopped crying, even if her life depended on it. She did her best, wiping away tears with the back of her hand, standing up straight. Her mother and grandfather looked at her through tearful eyes, full of sadness, pain, and something else she couldn't define. Now she spoke in Chinese, "I look after myself. Ma, Grandpa, I go…" No matter how hard she tried, she couldn't keep her voice from breaking. "I go now." With the last word and one last look at their tearful faces, she turned and left. There was a crowd of men, women, and very small children, who had seen and heard everything. Some of the women were crying or wiping tears off with their hands or sleeves. Most people, Chinese and Khmer alike, had looks of horror on their faces. But a few had smiles.

Without thinking, Moy said in Khmer, "Its travel around." With that, she walked painfully to where the headman was waiting, got on his bicycle, and was gone.

Moy lost track of time while she was on the bicycle and crying all the way. Then she found herself being helped down by the headman. He walked her into a big brown wooden house; there were about twenty or thirty children there. A few were crying and frightened like she was. There were about ten leaders, who were all dressed in black. They came to recruit more workers for their groups. Everyone looked clean except Moy.

Moy's light-blue flowered pants and yellow flowered shirt were blood-stained. Her feet were bare and covered in dry blood. Her face was smeared with blood and tears. The minute she walked in, some of the children made fun of her. They said she was acting like a baby and dirtier than a baby. But Moy didn't care. *I'll cry all I want. And no one can stop me. I wonder if they miss their families too, or have they become like Black Shirts and care only about the short-life Onka? Onka this and Onka that, everything is the short-life Onka!* Moy thought angrily.

A few minutes later, Moy found herself being carried in a black hammock by two big female leaders, who weren't happy with the job. They said she was as heavy as a pig and smelled like one too. The two girls were Khmers. They kept calling her all the names they could think of in their language, saying terrible things to her, "Chinese cloth, stupid Chinese, eat up all Khmer's rice. Go back to China! I hate Chinese cloth!" (These hateful words were a daily insult from some of the Khmer to the Chinese people in Cambodia.) Moy kept her mouth shut. The more they told her to stop crying, the harder she cried.

Moy didn't know how long they had been on the road when they passed the little mountain where she and Keem had worked; she turned her head sharply, taking a good look at it. As if she could read Moy's mind, the girl at the back of the hammock said, "If you run away and Onka catch you, Onka hit you away!" "Hit away" meant they would kill her. Moy turned to look at the girl and saw her lips were tight. Her eyes were hard. Her square face was filled with nothing but hatred. Moy's own lips were just as tight. Her eyes were just as hard, and her face held just as little love for the other, though it was lighter, dirty, and wet with tears.

"What you look at?" the girl shouted at Moy, who bit her tongue and turned away. *I must try to be nice to her. She might be my leader. If she hates me this much, there's no telling what she could do to me. I must keep some hope of going home. I don't know how I'll do it. But I'll be going home soon!* Moy thought.

17

Even if she found a way to escape, how could she walk home with her right ankle killing her like this? For the first time, she looked down at her right foot. It was swollen up as big as her head! Both legs were covered with dried blood, and blood was running down from her elevated ankle, all the way to her thigh. She tried to move, but she was trussed up in the hammock like a banana and her back was killing her. The girls yelled at her to be still or they'd make her walk. She tried her best to be still. *Where are they taking me?* she began to wonder and soon got her answer.

They stopped at a house with a metal roof and no walls—if you could really call that a house. Inside were about a hundred wooden poles with black or brown rice-bag hammocks tied to them. There were five or ten empty poles waiting. Moy guessed they were for the girls who were being taken away from their families today. In a short time, all the poles were filled up as other girls arrived.

Moy's brown rice-bag hammock was in the first line of the poles, on the edge of the wall-less building. Some of the sick girls there had tied it up for her, because they felt sorry for her. *These girls know who their mothers and father are. Not like the short-life Black Shirts, who love only Onka,* Moy thought. She thanked the girls for their help.

Moy lay in her hammock, crying her eyes out. About seven o'clock in the evening, the sun was still in the sky, and a large group of girls returned from work. She was half asleep, when she heard a voice that seemed to come from far away. Opening her eyes, she saw a big white face hanging over her.

"Wake up," the woman said softly. "Sleep like dead," she went on, smiling softly at Moy. Moy tried to get up and then moaned with pain. The woman looked at her with a frown, following Moy's eyes to her right ankle. The woman cried loudly, "Dead!" (Horrible.) She continued, "Her leg swollen to that size!"

She bent down further to take a better look and complained to someone behind her, "Why you take her? She sick. I want people come here to work. I want people who can walk. Why they send me this sick one?"

"Buddy Big Sister, she not sick. She just lazy," a girl said from behind the woman.

"Look at her leg! She hurt!" the woman shouted angrily to the girl behind her. No matter how angry the woman was, her voice sounded sweet to Moy's ears. "Get her some rice to eat," the woman told one of the girls. "I want you take her to hospital tomorrow. Now get some water for her to wash her face, hands, and feet."

As the woman turned away, Moy thought she saw some pity on her face. *She's pretty and kinder than the others,* Moy thought. The woman looked to be in her early twenties; she was dressed all in black like the Black Shirts. Her hammock was about five poles away. Moy watched her back as she sat in it, eating.

Soon, one of the girls brought some water in a bucket for Moy to wash with. The girl didn't say anything but gave Moy an odd look. When Moy was done, she took the bucket away. When dinner was over, the girls went back to work again. Moy sat looking at the meal on her plate: dry, cooked rice mixed with small green bananas and two small fish on top. Moy wasn't hungry. But she knew her mother would want her to eat. "Eat what they give you to stay alive, one day a time." *That's what Ma would say, if she were here,* Moy thought through tears, eating the rice with her fingers. Her hand shook; her throat was too tight to swallow, but her tears softened the rice to make it go down her throat. *I won't eat the dried fish. I'll keep it. I'll give it to Grandpa and Ma when I get home,* Moy thought.

After dinner, Moy lay down on her brown hammock and cried herself to sleep. Sometime in the night, she heard two people talking.

"Pity her. Her leg swollen this big. It must hurt," said a soft voice.

A girl with a louder and bitter voice said, "Buddy Big Sister, you good heart. You pity everyone."

"I pity *her!* You carry her to hospital tomorrow. They not have anything to give her, but take her there anyway," said the soft voice. Moy didn't know who the voice belonged to, and she didn't care. All she cared about was going home. *And that will be soon,* she assured herself.

Moy couldn't sleep that night. As she lay in her hammock with eyes open wide, tears were her best friend; they understood what she longed for. She longed for her mother's arms to wrap around her and comfort her. She longed for her mother's voice whispering in her ear, "You cold?" If she nodded yes,

Keem would pull Moy closer to her, keeping Moy warm. If Moy shook her head no, Keem would ask, "You can't sleep? What you think about?" If Moy didn't answer, her mother's hand would be on her forehead to see if it was hot, and she would peer down at her daughter's face and ask, "You all right?" When Moy smiled at her, Keem would cry out, "Flat-nosed lady!" then pat her small nose lightly and say, "Go to sleep!"

Oh! How she longed for her mother. But she wasn't there to comfort her. Moy tried to comfort herself by thinking of other things her mother had told her. But she couldn't think of one. All she could think of was, *I want Ma. I want to go home to Ma!* Then she started to cry harder, covering her mouth with her hands, so she wouldn't wake the others. Her hammock shook from her hard sobbing, and she cried until there were no tears left to come. Then she just lay in her hammock and looked up at the black sky. The sky was so dark, but the full moon was bright. And thousands of stars shone down at her. *Dark and bright, black and white, twinkling but high. Now it is the dark side of my life, to live without Ma and Grandpa. All the love, care, and understanding they have given me. That has been the bright and shining part. In the past, when they have punished me for doing something wrong, that was the black part. When they let me have my own way if I was good, that was the white part. And the goals they set for me are high and hard to reach. But the pride on their faces and twinkles in their eyes when I achieve them. Only one life to live, but I've seen all this.*

Moy pulled herself out of her thoughts and looked around the area. Every once in a while, she would see two or three Khmer Rouge walking up and down on the footpath, not far from the building. Each of them carried a long gun, either over his shoulder or in his hands, ready to fire. Now and then, one of the guns would go off, sometimes for no good reason and at other times, perhaps to frighten the hungry wolves away. But none of the exhausted girls was awakened by it.

Watching the Black Shirts, Moy understood what that no-good girl meant when she said, "If you dare run away, Onka hit you away!" She hadn't lied. These Black Shirts were shooting off their guns for fun; they would shoot a runaway without a second thought. They would shoot anything that moved or got in their way. *I can't go home now,* Moy thought. *It's no good if I go home dead. Ma would kill herself over that. But I want to go home. No matter how many guns they have, no matter how many Black Shirts are here. If I want to go home, I'll go home. All the Black Shirts in Cambodia can't stop me! Home, here I come!* At this last thought, Moy's lips softened a bit and then smiled slowly. Then she closed her eyes…

18

When Moy opened her eyes again, the sun was high above her head. The girls had returned from work again to eat lunch. Sweat poured down their faces. If the heat didn't kill them, their clothes would. It was somewhere around 100 degrees, and every one of them wore a black sarong and black long-sleeved shirt. Every girl was grateful to get into the shade of the building. Everyone wanted water more than anything else. Some yelled and shouted at others not to drink too much and to leave some for the rest. Others were fighting for water, swinging their fists and pulling each other's hair, screaming and crying. Moy turned her head away to block out the noise. *They can fight till the mountain falls on their heads. I don't care,* she thought.

Looking toward the road, she saw three lines of boys coming out of the deep forest. Each carried a long hunting knife or ax on his shoulder. Each boy wore long black pants and a black long-sleeved shirt. A few Khmer Rouges walked next to the lines of boys, guns on their shoulders or in their hands. None of the boys was talking or laughing. *They acted like prisoners in the movies!* Moy turned to look at the girls again, wondering if they were treated the same way. But what she saw was the fighting and screaming. Then suddenly, two big Khmer Rouge women with guns appeared.

Moy watched without blinking. The two big women and the headwoman were trying to pull the fighting girls apart. When that didn't work, one of the big women took her gun from her shoulder, pointed it toward the sky, and fired two or three shots. Everyone stopped where they were, wide-eyed.

"You get us all kill!" some girls cried.

"Quiet! Quiet!" the Khmer Rouge women shouted, both pointing their guns upward and firing two or three shots. Everyone was quiet. Not a sound could be heard. Tears were streaming from everyone's eyes, even the headwoman's.

Horrified, Moy turned her face away, only to see fifteen or twenty men with guns come running toward the girls' building. Their guns were in the position to shoot. Their faces were as hard as stone. Their lips were set tight, and their dark eyes were filled with hatred. They ran in all different directions, as if they were taking an enemy camp. When they had surrounded the building, they stopped, guns aimed at the girls. *If they shoot, I will be the first to go,* Moy thought.

Moy couldn't move, couldn't even blink her eyes. All she could do was stare into the stony dark face nearest to her. His eyes were red above his high cheek-bones, small mouth, and chin. His long gun was pointing very close to her. She couldn't hear or see anything but the man and the gun. She didn't know how long she stared like that. Then his face turned soft. She saw his lips move, though she couldn't hear what he was saying. Then she realized another face was peering at her. Blinking her eyes few times, little by little, she began to hear their voices.

"She scare to death!" one of the men said, and they all laughed.

"Look! Her face white like dead people," said another, and they laughed more loudly.

"Good she scare like that!" one of the women said bitterly.

"Don't be scare, Buddy Little Sister! Buddy big brother not shoot you away." All of them laughed loudly. Then one by one, they walked away from the girls' building, still laughing.

"Pity her," Moy heard one of the men whisper softly.

"Onka not pity anyone!" one of the women snapped back.

"I say play, Buddy Big Sister!" said the man, meaning he was just joking, and they all laughed again.

Moy felt as if she had died and been born again. *I'll remember this as long as I live,* she thought. *But I won't tell Ma and Grandpa about it when I get home.*

One of the girls brought her some food. Moy ate the dry cooked rice with small green bananas, not caring much about anyone or anything, but she took the dried fish and wrapped them in the banana leaves and put them in her small clothes bag, saving them for Ma and Grandpa.

She wasn't sure what time it was when four girls told her to get out of her hammock. She did. They tied the hammock to a long stick and told her to get in again. Two girls picked up each end of the stick and prepared to carry Moy off to the hospital, wherever that was. They walked for a long time. The girls took turns carrying Moy in the hammock.

Moy nearly jumped out of the hammock with joy when she saw *that small mountain,* where Keem would be working on the other side. The girls yelled at her to be still or they'd make her walk. Soon, they did, nearly breaking her back when they dropped the hammock. Moy cried out from the pain in her back and leg, but the girls only laughed at her. She could hardly stand up, because her right ankle was killing her. The minute she stood up, blood started to flow from the wound on her ankle. Every step she took, she cried out aloud. She didn't know whether it was from the pain in her leg or the joy that she felt at being so close to home.

"Walk faster!" one of the girls yelled at her, giving her a hard shove on the back. Moy fell facedown on the hot road and started to cry harder.

"Stop torture her! You not know how to pity her? You hurt someday, and someone treat you the same!" one of the biggest girls shouted at the one who had pushed Moy.

"Buddy good heart! Why not you carry her yourself?" the girl snapped back.

"When we go back, I tell buddy big sister on you!" The threat to tell the headwoman shut the girl up nicely.

"Get up!" the big girl shouted at Moy.

Moy tried but fell back again from the pain in her leg. The girls put the hammock close to her on the ground, and Moy crawled into it. They picked it up and carried her again.

A bit later, they got to the hospital. The doctors and nurse came out to meet them at the gate. Moy had a horrible time telling the doctors from the nurses. They all dressed in black, just like all the girls and boys who worked in the field from which she had just come. Moy was used to seeing doctors wear white. Now she couldn't tell who was who. But she really didn't care as long as they didn't kill her. All she wanted was to go home.

They gave her a small metal bed to sleep on. As for meals, they gave her a dipper of thick rice soup and a spoon of salt for lunch and dinner. She ate the soup but saved the salt for Ma and Grandpa. They had been running short of it at home. She wrapped it in a piece of white paper and put it into her small clothes bag.

The Khmer Rouge doctor gave her salt water and a small cloth to cleanse her infected ankle three times a day. They gave her black, brown, and whitish pills to take. The pills were made from tree bark. Moy threw them all away when she went to the forest to relieve herself. They tasted sweet and were supposed to be good for everything—stomachache, headache, foot infection, you name it! *They are just too good. I wonder why Black Shirts don't give them to the dead to bring them back to life!* Moy smiled sadly.

The hospital was full of sick people, women and girls at one end, men and boys at the other end. Everyone had the same size bed and ate the same food. No one laughed or talked much. On the fourth day, Moy went outside the main building and noticed for the first time that it was made of white cement, flanked by two long brown houses, where the Khmer Rouge doctors lived. She looked longingly toward the mountain. *I want to go to Ma, and I will go very soon,* she thought through her tears.

That night, Moy went out again and sat in front of the building looking at the mountain, as if staring at it long enough would bring her home to Ma and Grandpa. Without thinking, she got up and started toward the gate with painful steps. But after only a couple of steps, someone shouted at her, "Buddy, go where?"

Moy turned her head and saw three women with guns sitting in front of the brown houses. Without thinking, she shouted back, "I see something bright, bright over there!" She pointed a finger in the direction of the gate.

She heard the women laugh, and one of them said to her, "Buddy want to run home. Get in before I shoot buddy away!"

Moy didn't say another word but walked back slowly and painfully, tears falling from her eyes. *Black Shirts won't stop me from getting home to Ma and Grandpa,* she thought angrily.

19

For nearly two weeks now, Moy had been separated from her beloved mother and grandfather. And she had nearly gone crazy from missing them. Without a second thought, she pulled her pants and shirts from the small clothes bag and took them into the forest, where she tore them and made holes here and there. When she was done, she returned to the main building and put her clothes back into the small bag. Then she went to the desk near the front door and asked the high and mighty Black Shirt doctor if she could go home and get some needles to mend her torn clothes.

The doctor told her sweetly, "Onka have many needle here in hospital. Onka give buddy some."

The black-hearted creature dared smile at her. Moy felt as if she were being kicked in the face, and her blood ran cold. She felt like crying but fought back tears and said as innocently as she could, "But I need more clothes. Onka give me no clothes to wear. Onka not like me go around with no clothes on."

"Buddy right! Onka not like that! But Onka have many clothe to give buddy some to wear."

That no-good black heart keeps smiling at me, Moy thought angrily, her blood as hot as the summer sun. *How I'd like to put my nails on his face!*

"I need mosquito net!" The words slipped out before she knew what she was saying.

"Onka also have mosquito net to give buddy," the young doctor replied, continuing to smile at her.

"Onka not give me any!" Moy nearly shouted at him. *That dog heart keeps showing me his white teeth, but his heart is black like night.* Then she realized he was toying with her. And she just stood there and looked at him. He was about her brother's age but smaller and shorter. He seemed to be waiting for her to argue with him. When she didn't, he seemed disappointed. He got up and went off somewhere. Moy waited; she wasn't sure how long she stood there before he returned.

The doctor chuckled softly to himself and handed her a piece of white paper. He went to sit on his chair behind the desk. Still smiling, he told Moy, "Two day. Come back yourself. Or I send buddy sister and buddy brother to drag you back."

They stared at each other, both knowing Moy would never come back. Now Moy really felt like crying but managed to whisper softly to him, "Thank you, Buddy Big Brother."

"What?" he shouted, leaning closer.

"Thank you, Buddy Big Brother."

"Two week, first time I see you smile," he said, eyes dancing.

Moy turned away quickly, fingers on her lips. *I smiled at that no good black heart? He wouldn't say so if I didn't. That...good heart Black Shirt!*

Moy went to her bed and picked up her small clothes bag, put it on her shoulder, and walked painfully up to the young doctor at his desk. Moy stood in front of his desk and waited until he looked up. She stared into his eyes and told him, "I wish buddy big brother have long life." With that, she walked out of the main building.

She had almost gotten to the gate when the Khmer Rouge, two women and three men with guns, stopped her and asked where she was going. She showed them her pass. They gave her a long, hard look. The men looked at her oddly, but she didn't care how she looked. All she cared about was going home to see Ma and Grandpa again. Moy held her breath. After a long moment, one of the men told her to go. *Home! I'm going home!* she cried to herself with joy.

Tears of joy, tears of pain, and tears of sorrow dropped from Moy's eyes. With every step she took, she left her pain and loneliness one step further behind. Taking the brown road to the left of the hospital, she walked for fifteen or twenty minutes and then turned right and walked through the tall grass. After thirty or forty minutes, she was at the mountainside. Still crying with joy and pain, she kept walking no matter how much her ankle hurt. Every step brought her closer to her beloved mother and grandfather. Dark and bright, black and white, twinkling but high—she would get them all as soon as she got home. "Home! I go home!" she cried aloud in Chinese.

The walking was difficult. She hopped on one foot when her right ankle hurt too much. Since in the jungle there was no footpath, Moy pushed and walked through the tall thick grass on bare feet. Sometimes, she stepped on thorns. When that happened, she sat down crying, pulled the small thorn out, and got up and walked or hopped on. Short grass or dry leaves on the ground would brush her ankle, and she would sob aloud in pain, stop and wait until the pain had eased, and then go on. She was very happy when she passed the tall, sharp grass area. She broke off a couple of large leaves, wrapped them around her foot and ankle loosely, and tied it off with a tiny root to protect her wounded ankle. She walked and hopped faster along the mountainside. She kept alert eyes on where she was going, careful not to step on thorns or go near small sticks that might poke through the leaves and hurt her ankle. While walking, Moy begged Great-Grandma and Great-Grandpa's spirits through her tears to protect her from harm and help her get home quickly.

Nature took pity on the young girl. A white rabbit with long pink ears came out from behind a big tree and sat watching Moy as she walked by. She stopped, looked at the rabbit through her tears, and waved gently at it. It didn't run away as it should; it just sat there, cocked its head to one side, and looked at Moy, as if it understood her feelings. It looked down at the ground and then up at her again, as if it were saying good-bye and then turned slowly and was gone. But Moy wasn't lonely, because birds sang to keep her company along the way, and the hot summer breeze turned soft and sweet, blowing gently on her face to cool her on her long, hard walk. As if the bright, sunny sky understood the young girl's need for the pure water from heaven, it sent a few drops of rain to wash away her tears and the nightmare memories, of the past two weeks.

The sound of the wind and the song of the birds kept her company all along the mountainside. Moy walked through tall grass, around big and small trees, and over big and small rocks, but she never stopped. Not too far from where she had met the rabbit, she saw a small snake moving slowly across the path in front of her. She waited until it went by, not afraid of it or it of her. *Rabbit and snake, white and black*...But mainly, she was thinking of home right then.

She walked all morning and afternoon. It was nearly sundown when she reached the other side of the mountain. She was close enough to the work area to see some men, women, and children squatting or kneeling as they cut the small trees. But her tearful eyes shut out all but one person in the group: a woman with long black silk pants, a dark-blue short-sleeved shirt, and a red-and-white plaid shawl around her head. She sat on her heels, her left hand pulling on a little tree as she cut it with the ax in her right hand. Moy cried uncontrollably, as she recognized Ma.

She wanted to call out, but she couldn't find her voice; her throat was too tight. The only thing she could get out was more big teardrops from her eyes. She was close enough now to hear some of their voices. The she saw her mother's head come up slowly, and Moy's heart stopped. *She sees me now!* Moy hoped. But to her disappointment, Keem looked down again and swung her small ax harder at another little tree. A few minutes later, her head came up sharply, and she looked in Moy's direction. Keem froze for a moment and then got up slowly, still looking toward Moy. She started to move slowly toward her, as if she were afraid faster movement would make her daughter disappear.

Now, so close to her mother, Moy felt the pain in her ankle worse than any pain she had ever known. Moy's steps got slower and slower. Her voice was still locked in her throat. She felt so weak she could hardly stand up. She wanted to wave to her mother. But her hands were so heavy she couldn't even lift a finger but kept walking and hopping forward.

Keem's steps also grew slower. She walked as if in a dream, hands at her sides and eyes staring straight ahead not blinking. She was afraid to blink because she might wake up from her dream and be back in the nightmare.

Moy saw her mother's lips move and knew she was calling her name. But no matter how hard she tried, she couldn't get a sound to come out of her tight throat. Their steps grew slower and slower and brought them closer and closer. Moy looked past her mother and saw all the workers get up to their feet slowly. They all turned to watch the mother-and-daughter reunion, the moment of heartbreaking joy. Mother and daughter stopped a few yards from each other, eyes locked as if they couldn't believe their dream had come true.

Then Keem whispered softly with tears streaming from her eyes, "Moy...?" Keem spoke as if she were still in a dream. Moy just stood there looking at her beloved face, crying all the time. "Moy?" Keem whispered more loudly still unable to move.

Finally, Moy found her voice and screamed, "Ma!" crying even harder. Both hands reached out as she started hopping toward her mother in painful steps.

"Moy! My child!" Keem cried, hands outstretched as she ran toward her beloved daughter. "My pulse! My flesh! My child! My life!" In a second, mother and daughter wrapped their arms around each other tightly, crying with happiness. Keem knelt to embrace her small daughter. Moy wrapped her arms around her mother's neck. After few minutes, Keem drew back to examine her daughter's face, and then she pulled her closer, hugging her even tighter. They pulled back again and looked at each other's faces. Keem's hand came up to touch her daughter's face tenderly, as if she wanted to make sure Moy was real.

"You come home!" Keem spoke through tears, not waiting for a response. She got up, turned her back to her daughter, and squatted down. Moy climbed onto her back. Mother and daughter were on their way home.

As Keem walked by the field-workers, Moy saw some women were crying having seen their happiness. Moy heard some of them whispering in Khmer as Keem walked past, carrying her, "I never see anything so sad. Pity them!"

"Sad, but now they happy."

"Pity them, much!"

20

On the way home, Moy hugged her mother so hard in her happiness that Keem laughed through her tears. Keem told her to loosen her hold around her throat or she wouldn't have a mother to hug anymore. Moy laughed and loosened her hold. Keem walked through the trees and underbrush for few minutes and then entered the town. She squeezed her daughter's legs. She felt Moy grow tense with excitement, but neither said anything until they reached the house. Wong was sitting on his brown hammock.

"Dad, Moy come home!" Keem shouted happily.

"Moy?" Wong looked up sharply. His face lit up when he saw his granddaughter behind his daughter's back. "You come home!" he cried in a broken voice, his hands reaching out to her.

"Grandpa!" The minute Keem put her down, Moy went to him hugging him hard and crying.

"This morning, I tell your Ma, last night, I dream you come home today," Wong told his granddaughter, hugging her tight.

"You dream good," Moy told him.

All three had tears of happiness in their eyes. Then they sat on the bed, Moy secure between the two adults. She told them where the Black Shirts had taken her and some of the things that had happened but left out the guns part. She meant to tell them about the rabbit and snake too. But she was too excited and tired and forgot.

They talked for a while. Then Keem went out to find eight different flowers and some grass. She returned with them, put them in a bucket of water, and stirred it around with her hand eight times. Then she helped Moy undress and bathed her with the water to wash off her bad luck. Moy was still wearing the same clothes she wore the day she left. They were caked with dried blood.

This was the first time in two weeks that Moy had had a bath. Keem dried her daughter and dressed her in clean clothes. Then she washed the blood from the ones Moy had taken off.

At dinner, Moy took out the small dried fish for her mother and grandfather to eat. She gave them the two handfuls of salt she had saved. They cried when they saw the fish and salt.

"You fall down on sand and grab a handful up with you," Wong told her. These were his words of wisdom to his granddaughter.

That night, they were all very happy to be together again. Moy told them all over again about everything that had happened, except about the guns and the white rabbit and snake. Then Moy began drifting off to sleep but overhead them talking.

"She too thin! They want to kill my sad granddaughter!"

"I think she not eat what they give her," Keem said in a sad voice.

"Good child, not eat food they give her. But save those small fish for us. In future, we must give her good day," he said, meaning they must wish her a good future and good fortunate. "She too thin! Too thin!" Wong whispered in an unhappy voice.

"She smell very bad. She wear same clothes like the day she go."

"Smell or no smell. The important thing my granddaughter home. That what important!" Wong snapped at his daughter. They continued to argue softly, and soon Moy heard no more.

When Moy woke the next morning, the sun was high and bright. At first, she didn't know where she was. Then she remembered she was home! She turned to look for her mother. But she wasn't there.

"Ma?"

"She go to work," Grandpa told her from his hammock.

Moy smiled at the sound of her grandpa's voice. She sat up, rubbing her sleepy eyes with the back of her small hand and pushing her lower lip out. She got out of the mosquito net.

"Spoil child!" Wong said, laughing.

Moy put her hands down and smiled, looking at her grandpa, who sat in his hammock with his feet on the ground. *It is good to be home and to be a little girl again. Grandpa looks much thinner, and his face has no color.* She kept these thoughts to herself.

"Your ma love you, love you to death," Wong told his granddaughter. "She cry every day and every night for missing you. Every night, she cry herself to sleep."

Moy looked down at her hands on her lap. *I cried myself to sleep every night too,* she thought sadly.

"You must know your ma love you to death. In future, you must be good, good to her. Don't mistreat your ma when she get older. You must not mean and starve your ma, when she get older. Let her eat what she want. Don't make her sad. Make your ma happy; let her love you." These were to be his last words of wisdom to his granddaughter.

"Yes," Moy whispered not looking at her frail old grandpa. She vowed to keep that promise, for as long as she was able to see the sun shining above her head. In the meantime Moy told herself, *I'll do whatever Ma and Grandpa tell me. And never say no to their wishes, at any time.*

Not long after Moy had washed her face, her mother returned from work. They heard the lunch bell from the shared kitchen. Keem didn't let her daughter out of the house. She and Wong went to lunch. But each of them saved some of their share of the thin rice soup and brought it home for Moy. They were hungry but happy just to have each other.

Keem went to work on the mountain each day. Moy stayed home with Grandpa. Her right ankle was improving each day, because she cleaned it with the water used to rinse rice before cooking. But their happiness didn't last long. When Moy's ankle was almost healed, she started to get the same sickness as Grandpa. Every time she went to relieve herself, she passed blood and tissue. Then one day, nearly a month after her return home, what her beloved grandpa did nearly broke her heart. The memories would live in her mind and soul forever.

21

Moy was standing half in and half out, leaning on the door frame of the house. She had just come back from picking some long green beans for dinner. She was staring into space, thinking about nothing in particular, not even the sweat pouring down from her forehead and back. Then a slight noise pulled her back from her own world. She turned her head toward the house where the sound had originated. Moy watched her grandpa. He was on his hands and knees beside his hammock, facing the doorway.

"Ooo! Ooo!" he cried happily, his head turning left and right. He was looking intently at something in his palms. He was like a little boy with his first toy.

Moy stood where she was and watched with interest. Grandpa looked up smiling shyly, like a little boy who had been caught stealing candy from a jar. Boyishly, he opened his hands slowly, showing her what he had. A strange sound escaped from Moy's throat when she saw the teeny little baby mouse, still pink, its eyes not yet open. It was screaming in a tiny voice. Wong looked away shyly. Then he threw the baby mouse into the fire in the ground stove next to him. After a minute or two, he picked it up with two small sticks, put it in his palm, and blew on it to cool it off. Then he looked up at Moy, smiling like a little boy with a big piece of candy.

Wong smiled handsomely and asked shyly, "Yes? No?" He held both hands out to her, offering her the brown cooked baby mouse in his large palms, like a teeny little boat in the middle of the ocean. His eyes were bright. His smile was one that could leave women breathless. Moy felt her throat close up. She felt like screaming and crying at the same time at the sight of her beloved grandpa, so childishly happy over such a little thing. She left…helpless, and her knees threatened to give way.

"No," she whispered softly, not able to cry or find enough voice to scream. She couldn't even move to help her grandpa back into his hammock. She just stood there and watched helplessly, as he got into the hammock himself. He sat there bending down, turning his head this way and that, looking at what was in his hands, like he never wanted to forget what a cooked baby mouse looked like. After he had looked his fill, he slowly picked it up with two fingers and very carefully held it to his mouth.

Before he bit into it, he paused and looked at Moy. He asked with the teeny, cooked baby mouse at his lips, "You not want it?" He looked so hopeful, so handsome, so shy, and so much like a little boy. It just...it just broke her heart.

"No." She couldn't look away from him.

He lowered his eyes shyly and happily, slowly bit into the cooked baby mouse, and chewed long and thoughtfully. He ate it in four or five bites. This cooked baby mouse was no bigger than *her* little finger. He chewed very slowly and thoughtfully, as if he wanted to remember how each bite tasted. When he finished, he licked his fingers thoroughly and said like a little boy, "Sweet! Sweet! Good to eat!" He gave her a pleased smile.

Moy didn't know what to do or say. She didn't know whether she wanted to laugh or cry. She just stood there feeling helpless. "Yes," she whispered, her throat feeling tight.

After dinner that night, Moy was sitting on the ground in front of their house with her mother's arms around her. The night was beautiful. The moon was full and bright, and the sky was clear. Moy told her mother what had happened that day, while she was working. Keem didn't say anything for a while. Then she told Moy she should look away if it happened again, so Grandpa wouldn't feel embarrassed by her staring.

Keem also told Moy she must learn to back down sometimes. She couldn't always win. She told her daughter she was lucky that the Black Shirt who gave her the pass to come home didn't slap her for insulting him by looking into his eyes. Then they talked about one thing and another and ended up giggling softly, as Grandpa slept in his hammock.

"If I can pull the moon down for you, I pull it down for you," Keem whispered on Moy's head and tightened her arms around her daughter. "Hear me?"

"Yes." Moy smiled hugging her mother's arms in front of her. Every now and then, Keem would repeat these words to her daughter.

Then Keem told Moy something else that frightened the living daylights out of her. "Few night ago, I dream," Keem started in a sad voice, "I dream your grandpa die. And he have only his small blanket to cover him. But I see his five sign still good."

"Then he won't die!" Moy whispered. Knowing her mother had the gift of reading people's faces, using the five signs—red, yellow, blue, black, and white pigments—in a person's skin to read their futures. But Moy was sad at the thought of what might happen to Grandpa.

Keem didn't answer Moy directly. Instead, she said, "Your grandpa love you, love you to death. Sometime, he cry at night for missing you. He worry to death about you. He worry Black Shirt hurt you and torture you. Sometime, he call your name in his sleep. He tell me not to worry about you. But his heart ache because you not here. He love you to death. If anything good to eat, let him eat more. He old, and he not eat that much longer," Keem reminded her daughter. Moy was near to tears listening to her mother. Keem continued in a sad voice, tightening her arms around her daughter, "Be good, good to him. Your grandpa love you, and don't ever forget that!"

No, I won't forget. As long as there is an earth for me to walk on and the sun above my head for me to see, I won't forget Grandpa loves me, Moy thought. Mother and daughter sat quietly for a long time, their closeness giving them joy. That would be shattered all too quickly.

22
June 8, 1977

Moy heard a voice that seemed to come from very far away. Then it came closer and closer with each shout, and the voice became clearer and clearer. The voice belonged to her mother.

"Dad! Dad!" Keem screamed.

Moy got up quickly when Keem's voice broke and she began to cry.

"Dad! Dad! What wrong with you?"

Something is very wrong, Moy thought fearfully. She got out of the mosquito net as fast as she could and froze at the edge of the bed. Her mother was down on her knees next to Grandpa's hammock. She had her father's face between her shaking hands. She kept crying and calling to him, "Dad! Dad! What wrong with you? Dad, open your eye!"

Moy looked at her grandpa's face. His eyes were closed and his lips and face were light pink. He was smiling the most beautiful smile she had ever seen. He looked so young, so relaxed, so handsome. His face was clear of all worry and so innocent and handsome looking. It hurt Moy's eyes to look at him. But she just sat there looking at Grandpa Wong. She couldn't have moved if she had wanted to, so she just sat there staring at Grandpa Wong Lai's handsome face.

"Dad! What wrong with you? Don't do this! Dad, don't do this!" Keem was crying so hard her whole body shook and her voice became hoarse. She continued to kneel there, holding her father's face in her trembling hands.

Moy knew the answer but asked anyway, "Ma? What wrong with Grandpa?" Moy sobbed, dry-eyed, because she just couldn't find her tears.

Keem was crying so hard she couldn't answer for a few minutes. Then, as if her daughter's question had made her accept the truth, she whispered tearfully, "Your grandpa die now." She continued in a broken voice, "Go tell that Khmer. Tell him come help your grandpa."

Keem continued sitting there, holding her father's face. Moy slid out of bed and ran as fast as she could to Pon's house, which was about a five-minute walk away. A week earlier, Pon had walked his cow beside their house and stopped to talk to Keem. After that, he kept coming to see them. Sometimes, he brought them potatoes to eat. He had told them if they ever needed any help at all, they should let him know.

Moy didn't stop when she got to Pon's house. She just shouted that they needed help and ran back, not turning to see if he had heard her or not. She didn't know what to do when she got home again. She stood near the bed, looking at her grandpa, sobbing without tears as she listened to her mother cry. *Last night, he slept with his head toward the east, but this morning, his head is pointing toward the west.* Moy looked at his legs, which were hanging out of the hammock; there were a few small red ants on his badly swollen feet. Her mother's hands swatted angrily at them, as if she were saying, "How dare you harm my father!" Keem seemed to be off in her own sad world, unaware of anyone besides herself and her beloved father's dead body.

When Pon got there, he stood next to Moy and said in a sad voice, "He smile very pretty. He die very pretty." With that, he helped Keem stand up. Then he left for few minutes and returned with two other Cambodian men. The three men and Keem picked Wong's body up and laid him carefully on his side of the bed. Still crying, Keem went outside to get a bucket of water. She knelt close to her father on the bed. She removed the long, thin towel that was all he wore, every day and every night. It was easier for him when he needed to go and relieve himself so many times a day. She washed him with a clean towel dampened with water. As she washed him, she kept calling to her father, as if she could call him back to life again.

When she finished, Keem looked through his bags to find his newest clothes. She dressed him up in long, dark-blue pants and a white, long-sleeved shirt. In all his sixty-two years, he had known no other color of shirt. Keem combed his black hair to one side, the way he liked. Then she put his heavy eyeglasses in his shirt pocket, so he could see. She put his brown flip-flops on his feet, to help him walk in his next life. She also took out two handfuls of money, all five-hundred ning bills and put them in his folded hands, so he would have money to spend.

95

Moy watched from the doorway, still sobbing without tears, as Keem continued to cry.

"His face still warm and pink. He not die?" Keem asked the men hopefully, tears dropping from her cheeks.

"The man die!" one of the big men nearly shouted at Keem.

He wasn't happy to be there; Moy could see that. But she didn't say anything. What could she say? That no man should die this happy, because he had eaten a cooked baby mouse the day before? That no man should be forced out of his hometown to die in this forsaken forest? Would the big man understand that? No. He wouldn't understand. No man could understand.

"The human stiff. Stiff like wood! When human stiff like wood, human die!" the big man shouted at Keem.

"Why you shout at her? Her father die, and you shout at her! You not pity her?" Pon yelled at the big man.

But Keem didn't even seem to know the men were arguing. Then Pon sent the two men to tear a section of wall off an empty house to serve as a stretcher. The men returned with a section of wall about thirty inches wide and six feet long, made of bamboo trees bound together with roots. They tied a rope at each end of the wall section. Then they picked Wong's body up. Keem helped by holding on to her father's head. Together, they put Wong Lai's body on the bamboo stretcher.

Moy looked at her grandpa's beloved face for the last time. But still no tears would come. *He looks so much younger than his sixty-two years, so free and so happy to go,* Moy thought with a heart shattering into millions of pieces. *Just a little meat, from that baby mouse, and he is happy to go. Men should have a lot of money and big beautiful houses to live in to be this happy. But not my poor grandpa.*

Only an unselfish, kind, and understanding man like Mr. Wong Lai, could die this happy and free of care with so little—a man like Mr. Wong Lai, dying in a hateful land among its unkind people. But he smiled at them and died happy, because he had defeated them all! No more torture, pain, or suffering for him. They had insulted him when he was alive, but he was a kind and forgiving person, and he had taken no hatred with him. He had forgiven them all. Mr. Wong Lai was the best kind of human being that ever walked upon Mother Earth and beneath Father Sky. And now he was high and free from harm and injustice, free like a great beautiful *white hawk*, free like the *sweet wind*, free to go to his new kingdom in heaven, which was waiting for its king to return. He smiled because Father Sky was blue and clear. And His Highness the Sun was shining down to welcome him. He smiled because his *sweet* knights, the winds, had come to escort him to his new kingdom, and he smiled because he was taking the memories and his love for Keem and Moy along with him to his new kingdom. His knights would protect him from all harm, and so he smiled, because he was full of joy and happiness and free at last.

23

Moy stood like a piece of wood, watching her tearful mother cover Wong up, with his small brown-and-white plaid blanket, like it was in Keem's dream. The men picked up the ropes at each end, ran a long wooden pole through them, and carried Mr. Wong Lai's body out of the house. Keem followed behind, crying, "Dad! Dad! What we do without you?"

Moy stayed home with Pon's wife and daughter. She sat on the edge of the bed, mourning without tears. *Grandpa's not dead!* her heart screamed over and over. *How can he die? He can't die!* She cried to herself. She remembered when she was five and had had a toothache. Grandpa had carried her back and forth around the house all night as she cried her eyes out. Not once did he get impatient with her. He soothed her with soft words and told her how much he loved her. He even managed to say or do something to make her laugh through the pain of her toothache. *Who will carry me round the house now when I have a toothache?* She remembered those treats each day in Siem Reap and in Pailin. *Who will buy me flavored ice balls now? Who will take me to eat pork noodles every morning? He just can't die!*

"Her face white like ghost," Moy heard one of the women say. "She too sick and broken heart to cry with tear. Pity her."

It was nearly sundown when Moy heard her mother's tearful voice outside the house. As soon as Keem walked into the house, the women left. Mother and daughter started packing their belongings. As they packed, Keem cried; her tears could have watered a whole desert, but Moy's eyes were as dry as the sand on the mountaintop.

Keem and Moy moved out of the house, getting away from the sad memories, and went to live almost directly across the street in a different block, ruled by a different headman and with a different shared kitchen. Everything was different from the block Wong had lived in. The town had a few hundred houses arranged in three long lines. All the houses were rectangular, with walls of wooden boards, bamboo, or grass-covered sticks. The house Moy and Keem moved into had belonged to someone whose family had run away from the town to live elsewhere. The new house was about three or four feet above the ground, built of beautiful wooden boards. It had a good-sized metal door and a roof of brown grass. Within a few yards of the front door, there were coconut trees lining the sidewalk and along the street. The old farmer had probably planted the coconut trees before the Khmer Rouge took over. The water well was just a short walk away.

Inside Moy's new house, the bed was big. It nearly filled the whole house. From the door entrance to the bed was a three-foot-wide hallway. Close to the right wall, there were three big rocks on the ground, which were used as a cooking stove. There were water buckets, pots, and pans placed against the side wall, close to the cooking stove as well. About a foot away from the ground cooking stove were the three long wooden steps leading up to the bed. The bed was almost like a house in itself. It had three walls against it. The door was next to the bed, on the left. It was a good-looking house, but mother and daughter were not happy.

Moy and her mother put their belongings against the left wall. On the right wall, they put Wong's Spirit Stand—a rice can containing the incense burned during the prayers at his death, the place where his spirit would be. Keem and Moy slept in the middle, with their heads to the east and feet to the west. Keem's unhappiness was from losing her father, but Moy's was not only from losing her grandpa but also from seeing her mother so sad and hurt. Buddha…was she helpless! Moy didn't know what to do when her mother kept on crying and calling, "Dad! Dad!"

Moy went to the shared kitchen at the other end of town to get their share of food. She brought back thick rice soup and banana tree soup cooked with some sort of meat. But no matter what Moy did, she couldn't get Keem to eat.

"If something happen to you, who look after me?" Moy cried.

Keem seemed to get the message, but ate only a few spoonfuls. Then she started crying all over again, as Moy watched helplessly.

After a few minutes, she told Moy in an angry voice, "You know? Two knife chop at each other. Weak one go and strong one stay."

"What that mean?" Moy asked, looking at her mother's sad face.

"You and Grandpa have same sickness. It like two knife compete with each other. Weak one go, and strong one stay." With that, she broke down and started crying harder.

24

Moy couldn't help feeling guilty over what her mother had said. *It would be all right for Ma, if I had gone and not Grandpa,* she thought sadly, as she lay in bed next to her weeping mother. *I don't know what to do to make Ma stop crying. I wish I had some power to bring Grandpa back, but I don't. I don't have tears for him, though I love him. I cry without tears for Grandpa. I must not be a good granddaughter to him. I'm not a good granddaughter.* Moy remembered what he had told her a week before he died. "In the future, you cause my death!" He had shouted loudly in front of Keem. Moy didn't remember what she had done or said to make him so mad at her.

Keem told her daughter Grandpa was too sick to know what he was talking about. "Prove him wrong, and be a good granddaughter to him."

Moy had promised her mother to do this, but she had failed. *I have proved him right. I caused his death,* Moy thought. Even with that thought, she found no tears. That night, Moy was awakened many times by her mother's sobbing. She didn't know what to say or do. She had caused Grandpa's death. What could she say to her mother?

Moy turned to hug her mother, telling her not to worry. She promised to take care of her when she grew up. But none of this did any good.

Instead, Keem turned around and shouted at her, "Don't worry? You look after me? Your Grandpa just die. And don't worry." Keem turned her back on her daughter.

Yes. There is a lot to worry about. A lot of worry. I caused Grandpa's death. Moy withdrew her arm from around her mother's waist. She wasn't sure if Keem wanted her anymore.

In the next two days, Keem found a small piece of board. She wrote Wong's name on it in Chinese with a black pen. Three days after Wong's death, Keem and Moy went to visit his grave. It was the Chinese custom to pay their respects. Moy trembled with fear, listening to her mother howl. Moy watched Keem put that small piece of board with Wong's name on it at the head of the grave, serving as a headstone.

They brought cooked rice and some meat. But they didn't have the three pieces of incense, so they burned three blades of dry grass instead. As they knelt to pray, Moy was still dry-eyed. But Keem kept crying and yelling, "Dad! Dad!" like she was begging the grave to open up for her to jump in, join her father, and be happy again. The way her mother was screaming made the hair on the back of Moy's neck stand upright. She trembled in fear.

It is nothing like what a real grave should be, Moy thought. The soil still looked newly dug and mounded up, about five inches above the ground. It was covered with pine trees to keep the wolves from digging up and eating the body. The grave was on top of a little hill and close to two big trees. On the west border was an area of open grassland. In the other three directions, there were only trees and underbrush. Moy felt cold sweat running down her back, as she looked at the wilderness that surrounded her grandfather's grave.

Moy lost count of how long they had been there. Finally, she couldn't stand it any longer. She took her mother by the arm and said they must go home now, because the sun was almost set. They left the grave in the deep forest and headed home. On the way, they stopped at a small stream that ran down the hillside, where Keem washed her face and Moy took a drink. Keem cried all the way home.

Keem was not the same person after Wong's death. And things got worse after they visited his grave. Keem got sick. She became sicker and sicker as each day went by. Moy couldn't tell what kind of sickness she had. Keem ate and drank less each day. On the fifth day after Wong's death, Moy was awakened early in the morning by a loud noise.

Moy flew out of the bed and saw her mother lying facedown on the ground, half in and half out of the doorway. Next to her, a big metal bucket had overturned, spilling its contents on Keem and on the ground. The child screamed in horror, seeing her mother like that. She knelt beside her Ma and tried to pick her Ma up with her small arms, as big, fat tears rolled from her eyes.

"Ma! Ma! What wrong with you? Help! Help! Someone help me!" Moy screamed over and over in Khmer. It seemed an age had passed and still no one came to help.

Then Keem's eyes opened slowly and stared at her like she was a stranger. Her question shocked the life out of Moy.

"Who are you?" Keem whispered weakly.

"Ma, it me, Moy!" Her daughter spoke brokenly, crying hard. She held her mother's face between her hands. "Me, Moy, your daughter."

Keem stared at her daughter for a minute longer. Then her face softened a bit, and she whispered, "Ah, Moy."

By then, one of the Cambodian men was at the front door. Almost stepping on Keem's feet, he asked, as if he were blind, "What happen? Why you shout so loud and wake me up?"

"Uncle, help!" Moy asked in Khmer, addressing him with a title of respect. "Help my mother! Please help, Uncle!" She cried hard and held on to her mother.

The two of them managed to pick Keem up and get her back to bed. When the man left, Moy sat with her mother, crying in fear. Then she told Keem she needed to wash her off and get her dry. Moy got a big bucket of water from the well and brought it to the bed. She undressed her mother and used a large metal bowl to get water out of the bucket. She poured water over her mother's head slowly. She washed her mother's hair and body. After drying her with a towel, she dressed her mother in dry clothes. Then she moved Keem to the other part of the bed, where it was dry. After Keem slept for a few hours, she opened her eyes and saw her daughter's tearful face hanging over her.

"Ma! Oh, Ma! I scare to death!" Moy spoke with difficulty. She was very happy to see her mother's eyes open again and not staring at her like a stranger.

"Don't cry, crazy child," Keem teased her daughter weakly and smiled at her. Keem's loving smile made Moy cry even harder. "You eat yet?" Keem asked.

"No, I not want to leave you, Ma," Moy told her mother, while wiping tears off her face with the back of her hands.

"Go get our share of food. I be all right," her mother told her softly, closing her eyes again. Moy looked at her mother's beloved face for a minute longer and went to get the food. As soon as the food was dished into the metal pots, Moy headed home again as fast as her legs could take her.

She knew something was wrong when she got home. Moy couldn't explain what it was, but her mother's face didn't look right. "Ma? Ma?" she whispered as softly as she could.

"Yes?" Keem answered weakly, opening her eyes slowly.

"Eat rice," the girl told her mother, worry on her face, but love in her eyes.

"I not hungry."

"You must eat a little."

"I not hungry."

"Just one mouthful." *When you get up, I'll make you eat more than that,* Moy thought. And she did! She made Keem eat a whole bowl of rice soup and some dried fish. That night, they both slept peacefully. In the morning, her mother seemed stronger, like her old self again. Moy's sickness was also getting better. *I can't ask more than this,* Moy thought happily.

After lunch, Moy asked her mother to mend the pants she had torn on a small branch when she went to get food from the shared kitchen. Keem sat up in bed, looking strong, and sewed the torn pants. Then she lay down for a nap. Before she closed her eyes, she asked Moy to go to the old house to pick some long green beans for dinner.

Moy headed for the old house with a basket and a small knife. *But somehow she lost the knife on the way.* She picked two handfuls of the long green beans and was about to leave, but she changed her mind and went to stand in the doorway of their old house. Grandpa's brown hammock was still tied to the poles at the corner of the bed. Moy looked at the bed that Grandpa, her mother, and she used to share. Grandpa's small mosquito net used to be attached to the right wall. They stored their belongings against the left wall. Moy and her mother's larger mosquito net was attached to the left wall and the long pole over their heads and feet. The three-rock stove was on the ground, just three feet from their bed. They didn't have a door in this old house. *There were laughter, smiles, and happiness in this old house and...heartbreak too,* Moy thought. *But the house is empty now and life must go on.* She turned around and went home to the new house where she would see many things she didn't like in the days to come.

25

Keem was sitting on the bed, her knees drawn up under her chin, her back against the wall facing the door, when Moy got home. She smiled when she saw her daughter. Moy smiled back, glad to see her mother looking like her old self again. She went to sit on the step to the bed and told her mother *she had lost the knife*. Quickly, the look on Keem's face changed from love and joy to hatred and anger. She shouted at her daughter in a voice Moy had never heard before.

"You lose everything! Bad child! Good child bring water to bed, for her sick mother bath without fall to death!" Keem seemed to feel no pity for her sobbing daughter but continued to shout at her, "You not worth it! Worthless child! You not know anything. You will cause my death!" With that, Keem turned her back on her daughter. She crawled to the middle of the bed and lay down, ignoring her daughter, who was sitting on the step to the bed crying. But a few minutes later, Keem called to Moy in a soft, caring voice and told her to come sit next to her. Moy prayed the worst had past. She could not have been more wrong.

It got even worse that night. Grandpa's big, deep voice came out of Keem's mouth. He said he would take Keem with him, and they would go and live in Angkor together. Moy begged and begged the voice of her grandpa not to take her mother, because she was young and needed her. The whole night, Moy sat close to her mother, who talked with different voices. She often couldn't understand what they were talking about. One voice went out, and another voice came in—it kept getting worse.

After that, Keem was not the person Moy knew as her Ma. She started to talk more and more in strange voices. Her eyes had no light in them anymore; they were dark and dead. They would become brighter only when she spoke in her own voice. But that was happening less and less often. Keem was sick to the point that she couldn't get up anymore. Whatever she ate or drank, even water, she threw up almost immediately. Moy wasn't afraid of the voices and kept talk-ing to them. But she always looked at her beloved mother's face. Moy never left her mother's side, except to go relieve herself or to the shared kitchen for food.

On the seventh or eighth day, Keem asked Moy for a small hand mirror. Keem lay in bed. She examined her own face, turning the mirror this way and that. A funny sound escaped from her throat. "I near death now," Keem whis-pered. Moy burst into tears when she heard that. Keem continued to examine her face in the mirror. Then she put it down and looked at her crying daughter. She said, "Don't cry. I say play. Ma all right, nothing wrong with me."

"Nothing wrong with you," Moy said through tears. But she knew it wouldn't be long now. She had overhead Pon's wife say that to her daughter the day before, when she came to help out.

"Her hair all straight. Pity her. She not live long now." Pon's wife stopped as soon as she realized the girl had overheard. Moy sat crying silently, as she squat-ted near the stove cooking thin rice soup for her mother.

On the ninth day, Moy managed to get her mother to sit up and forced a few spoonfuls of rice soup into her mouth. Less than a minute later, she threw up everything. Immediately, the child brushed it away with her bare hands. *Hot... like fire.* Keem couldn't stand to see anything like that; she'd throw up at the sight, even when she was well.

"Child, in future, I give you good day," Keem offered her last wish for her beloved daughter.

"Yes," Moy whispered, understanding her mother was wishing her success and a better life in the future. She gave her mother some water to rinse her mouth and helped her lie down again.

That afternoon, Pon found a Cambodian witch doctor to see Keem, because she started to talk in different voices again. The witch doctor was a big, tall young man. He came empty-handed. He got up on the bed, sat next to Keem, and took her face in his hands. She went wild trying to fight him off and kept screaming in Khmer. No one but the witch doctor understood what the voice was saying. He said something in Khmer only the voice could understand. Keem screamed with horror, and her hands came flying at the witch doctor's face. Pon had to restrain her. Moy watched in horror, crying helplessly. As a Chinese girl, she couldn't understand what the witch doctor was trying to do to her mother.

Moy watched her mother, but she had no idea who this woman was. Keem had never spoken good Khmer, but the person lying on that bed was speaking it perfectly. She was fighting the witch doctor like a wildcat—her feet kicking; her

106

head tossing left and right; her eyes cold, angry, and hard. It was all Pon could do to hold her down, but the real Keem couldn't even sit up in bed without her daughter's help.

The witch doctor kept on whispering softly to her, looking into Keem's eyes when he could hold her head still. Suddenly, she gave out a ghostly scream and spit in his face. Then she was very still. The two men let go of her. After a few minutes, she opened her eyes slowly and looked around calling softly for her daughter in Chinese, in her own voice.

"Moy?"

"I here, Ma," Moy answered, still crying.

"Why these people here?" she asked weakly.

"They here to help you, Ma."

"You know me?" Pon asked hopefully in Khmer, leaning over her.

"I know you," Keem answered in Khmer.

"Good, good!"

But Pon spoke too soon. Wong's voice came out from Keem's mouth, speaking half in Chinese and half in Khmer. "I take Keem to live in Angkor with me. I love Keem, and I take her to live in Siem Reap where we happy together." Keem's eyes were closed; as she spoke, there was a beautiful and happy smile on her face.

Moy knelt close and addressed her grandpa's voice in Chinese. "Grandpa, you can't do this. I still very young, and I need Ma!" she nearly shouted.

Keem's eyes opened and looked at Moy with hatred. The voice asked angrily, "Who are you? I don't know you!"

"Grandpa, it me, Moy! Your granddaughter!" she shouted in Chinese.

"I not know this name. I take Keem to live in Angkor and happy together." The voice spoke in Khmer now.

"You take no one with you," the witch doctor said in Khmer from the other side of Keem. "Be happy ghost. Go to where you belong, and leave this body alone."

"I not afraid of you!" Keem pointed a finger at the witch doctor with a murderous look. The witch doctor held onto her finger and whispered something, and the voice screamed in fear. Keem's whole body began to shake violently.

"Now, let's talk. What you want and we give. Then you leave this woman's body alone. Yes?" the witch doctor asked slowly in Khmer. Keem's body was shaking in fear; she kept nodding, her eyes filled with horror. Moy felt bad for her mother, but she was very angry with Grandpa's spirit.

"I want to hear you say it," the witch doctor told the voice.

"Yes," the voice answered.

"Yes what?" the witch doctor demanded softly, but the voice became louder and more hostile. Keem pulled her finger from the doctor's grasp.

"Yes, I leave her alone!" the voice shouted at the doctor. Keem's body started to sit upright.

The witch doctor quickly grabbed onto her finger again, and she fell back like a helpless baby. The witch doctor asked with laughter in his voice, "You have power now?"

"Yes, yes, yes!" The voice sounded weaker now and always answered in Khmer. The doctor tightened his hold, and the voice screamed.

"And now?" the doctor demanded again.

"Yes!" the voice screamed.

"Now?" the doctor squeezed harder and laughed.

"Yes…no!" the voice shouted in pain.

"What you want?' the witch doctor asked.

"I want eat pig head," the voice said weakly. Keem's body didn't move, but her eyes looked at the witch doctor with hatred.

"No pig's head," the doctor told the voice.

"I want eat pig head!" the voice screamed.

"No pig's head."

"I want eat chicken," the voice shouted more weakly.

"What you do if I give you chicken?" the doctor wanted to know.

"I leave her alone."

"Leave who alone?"

"Keem, Keem, Keem!"

"You not take Keem if I give you chicken?"

"Yes."

"You leave her now. If I give you chicken tomorrow?"

"Yes."

"Now go! Not come back to harm this body again. If you come, I lock you up and you never free again. Agree?" The witch doctor's voice was like a king's, ordering his knights around and not taking "No" for an answer.

"Yes." Keem's face became soft, and the voice asked the witch doctor shyly, "Let me play here longer?"

"No! I want you go now!"

Keem gave the witch doctor a hateful look. Then her eyes closed slowly, and sleep overcame her.

Moy sat there watching and listening to the whole thing. Now that it was over, somehow, she didn't feel as relieved as she should have. She had the feeling something still wasn't right, but she didn't know what to say to or ask the witch doctor. Pon never said a word when the doctor was talking to the voice. He still didn't say anything, but he looked pretty scared. The men sat for a while looking at each other, saying nothing. Then the witch doctor took a bowl of water and ran his fingers around and around the rim a few times, whispering softly. He woke Keem up and made her drink the whole bowl of water, which she did without throwing up. Then he laid her back down again; she closed her eyes and slept quietly.

Before the men left, the witch doctor told Moy he would bring a chicken the next day and told her to pray to her grandfather. The men left. And the girl was alone with her sick mother. The girl didn't sleep but sat and watched her mother sleeping peacefully in the small light of the oil lamp, by the spirit stand. She didn't know what she felt. Love? Fear? Hate? Helplessness? Helplessness was more like it. Finally, she couldn't keep her eyes open any longer. She lay down next to her mother. The moment she closed her eyes, she was asleep.

Whom did the witch doctor make a deal with the voice to keep safe, Keem or Moy?

26

Sometime before the new sun was born, Moy was awakened by something cool hitting her face. She opened her eyes and was surprised to see her mother. Keem was sitting up next to the metal bucket of water by the wall. She was pouring water over her head with a small bowl, all her clothes still on. Moy lay there a second longer, watching her mother with a happy heart. *Ma can get up by herself!* Moy thought joyfully. Quickly, Moy got up and knelt next to her mother, putting both hands on her shoulders.

"Ma? What you do?" *Stupid, stupid question,* Moy told herself.

"I take bath! What you think I do?" Keem snapped at her daughter in a deep, loud voice, but it was *her* voice.

"Let me help," Moy offered softly and tried to take the metal bowl from her mother. But Keem pulled away angrily, holding on tight to the little bowl of water. "Ma, I have to take these clothes off and wash you." Both her hands held on to her mother's shoulders gently as she spoke. Keem turned to look at her daughter. Moy smiled with love.

"You wash me clean, clean?" Keem asked wide-eyed, like a little girl being offered a piece of candy.

"I wash you clean, clean." *I won't just wash you clean, clean; I'll even go jump off a mountain to get you to look at me like that again,* Moy thought with joy in her heart.

Keem looked a bit stronger, and her face was more relaxed; she was almost like her old self again. She let her daughter take the bowl of water from her hands and pull off her wet shirt. Then Moy moved her to sit with her back against the wall for support, while she pulled Keem's pants and underwear off. *She's too thin! Nothing but skin and bones!* Moy cried to herself. Moy couldn't help but stare at her mother's chest. She could count every bone with no difficulty. With an aching heart, she turned away. She didn't say anything to Keem. What could she say? Moy took the metal bowl from Keem's hands again, dipping water from the bucket and pouring it over her head. She washed her mother's hair and body with soap. Moy told her mother to close her eyes before she poured water over her head. Moy bathed her mother with the large bucket of water. Then she dried Keem off with a towel and moved her to a dry spot on the bed. She dried her off again and dressed her mother in clean clothes: underwear; dark-blue, short-sleeved shirt; and long black silk pants. Moy combed her mother's black shoulder-length hair.

When everything was done, Moy laid her mother down carefully on the dry side of the bed and let her go to back to sleep. Before Keem closed her eyes, her face was soft and a tiny *mysterious* little smiled played on her lips and face. Keem looked and looked at her daughter's face, as if she wanted to say something. But she didn't. She looked as if she wanted never to forget what her beloved daughter looked like. Then she closed her eyes and went to sleep without a word.

Moy looked at her mother's face and started to cry softly to herself. *I don't care if she yells and screams at me. I'd rather have her like this than not have her with me at all.* Moy sat there holding Keem's hand, looking her fill at her mother's face. Then she looked away slowly to the space between the wall and the roof and saw the sun was just peeking out a little. Moy couldn't go back to sleep. She got up quietly and tiptoed out of the bed space, taking her mother's clothes with her.

She took a metal bucket with a long rope to draw water from the well. No one was up yet; she had the well to herself. She carried the bucket back and set it down in front of the house. She then went to get the wet clothes. Before she picked them up from the step, she tiptoed up the steps to the bed to peek at her sleeping mother and make sure she was all right. Moy squatted on the ground in front of the door and washed the clothes in the bucket. But her ears were back in the house. If Keem made a sound, she could be next to her in no time.

She had almost finished washing the clothes when the witch doctor showed up with a small cooked chicken in a pot. Moy smiled at him when he got closer. He smiled back with pity in his eyes. He stopped in front of her and told her he wished he had a daughter like her. Moy smiled rather sadly at him. *If you knew me, you wouldn't want me this close to you,* she thought.

After Moy had spread the clothes on the bushes to dry, she went into the house. She started a fire and put some rice in the pot to cook. As part of the deal the witch doctor made to Grandpa's voice last night, she would offer dry cooked rice, a chicken, and prayer to Grandpa. While she cooked, the witch doctor sat on the bed next to Keem, whispering his witch doctor words softly in Khmer.

Moy had no idea what they meant, and she didn't care. All she wanted was for her mother to get better.

When the rice was done, Moy put the whole pot and the cooked chicken in front of her Grandpa's spirit stand. She took three small bowls and three pairs of chopsticks, which Keem had brought from Pailin. Moy put them next to the rice pot. She burned three pieces of grass in place of incense, knelt down before the spirit stand, and prayed. Moy begged Grandpa to leave her mother alone and help her get better soon. She asked him to bring good people to help them and chase bad people away from them. She knelt and prayed three times, waiting five or ten minutes in between, giving the spirit time to finish eating. She left all the food in front of the spirit stand, thinking that when Keem woke up she would force her to eat some of the rice and chicken and get stronger. Then they would be happy again.

But sometimes, dreams and hopes can turn into nightmares, friends into enemies, and truth into lies and betrayal.

27
June 18, 1977
3:00 p.m.

It was about noon when Keem opened her eyes again. She saw her daughter's smiling face above her. Keem didn't smile back but spoke in a weak voice to Moy.

"I want drink elephant water."

"I go find leave," Moy promised, telling Keem she would be right back. She knew where to find the plants with giant leaves that looked like elephant ears. She knew how to boil them into a drink and make it taste fresh. Chinese people believed it would keep a fever down. The plants were all over the place, in the forest and down near the small stream. She went to the forest and looked everywhere but couldn't find any! She went to the small stream but couldn't find a single elephant plant, not a single leaf! *What has happened to them? Has the whole world decided to drink elephant water every day?* Moy asked herself sadly. *Ma wants to drink elephant water, and I will find elephant plants!* She looked again, first down by the small stream and then back in the forest, but without success. After about an hour, she returned home and told her mother she hadn't been able to find the plants.

Her mother shouted at her furiously, "There lot of them around here! And you can't find any? Your mother near death! She want drink elephant water, and you can't find the plant? You worthless! Bad child!"

Moy didn't cry but felt shame and guilt; she looked at her mother for forgiveness. She knew the plants were all around, but she hadn't been able to find any. And there was nothing she could do about it. At lunch, Moy tried but couldn't force her mother to eat anything. She had a few bites of rice herself and felt guilty for being hungry. There was nothing she could do but sit next to her mother and watch her sleep. After a while, she felt so tired, she lay down next to Keem, throwing her small arm over her mother's chest, and fell asleep.

Moy didn't know how long she had slept, but she awoke with a pain in her stomach so severe she cried aloud. Hearing her mother moan softly, Moy drew her knees up to her chest. Wrapping both arms around her stomach, she said tearfully, "Ma? My stomach hurt." Moy was in agony with her stomachache.

"Whatever happen," Keem whispered weakly, pausing for breath before going on. "...let me receive them all. But let my child good, good," she said, meaning "let my child be well."

Keem's words were like magic. Moy's stomachache stopped as soon as her mother spoke these final words. Moy moved closer to her mother and fell asleep again. As soon as her eyes closed, *the dream began.* She saw Keem walking toward her, dressed in the clothes she had put on her right after her bath: the blue short-sleeve shirt and the long black silk pants. Keem's black hair was combed to one side, the way she used to wear it. Keem was smiling beautifully at her daughter. Moy's mother continued to smile without saying a word. Slowly, she turned her back on her daughter and walked off without looking back. The dream was so real, Moy wasn't sure she was dreaming.

Then...she heard *that noise,* and her eyes flew open. *It can't be!* She cried in horror to herself. She had heard *that noise* just a year before, when she saw a Cambodian woman die. *It can't be! She can't do this to me.* Moy lay paralyzed for a second longer, and then she jumped up to her knees, staring at her mother's lifeless eyes. Keem's mouth was open, and she was drawing in her last breath.

"Ma! Ma!" Moy screamed in terror. She jumped up and ran to look through the space between the wall and roof. Seeing Pon's granddaughter playing near the house, Moy shouted to her. "Go tell your father...my mother die!" The words just slipped right out from her lips. Moy saw the girl run off. She turned around and jumped off the bed, not caring if she broke her neck. She ran as fast as her legs would carry her to the witch doctor's house, screaming in Khmer as she ran, "Ma! Ma! Help me! My mother die! Help me! Help my mother! Buddha, help me!" Her cries and screams woke some people from their naps. They peered out from their houses to see what all the screaming and crying was about.

When she reached the witch doctor's house, she grabbed his big powerful arm and roused him from his nap, screaming, "Get up! Get up! Help my mother! My mother die! Help, help!"

The witch doctor sat up, still half asleep, and asked, "What?"

"My mother die! Uncle, help!" Moy screamed madly, dragging him by the arm. When it got through to him, he jumped to the ground and ran after Moy.

When they got to the house, Pon, his wife, and his daughter were already inside the house. A few hungry *vultures* were hanging around in front of the house and *waiting*. Moy went right up to the bed and sat next to her mother. People had already turned Keem around; her head was pointing to the west. Moy wanted to pull her mother into her arms and hug her. As she stretched her hands and arms out, Pon's wife yelled at her, "Don't touch her! Let her go in peace. Don't stop her and make her unhappy!" She paused and then continued, "Close your mother's eyes. She not close them when I try. And close her mouth too."

Moy's hand shook as she reached out to touch her beloved mother's face, for one last time. "Ma! Ma, don't run away from me! Buddha, don't take my mother. Give her back! Give her back to me!" Moy screamed at the top of her lungs. Her mother's face was cold. Moy tried to close her eyes and mouth, but they wouldn't close. She pulled her hand back. Moy looked skyward and stretched her hands toward heaven, hopping up and down on her backside and keening, screaming, and crying. "Buddha, I want my mother back! Buddha? Give me my mother back! I not have anyone, just me alone. Buddha, pity me. Please, give my mother back! Pity me, Buddha. Give me my mother back, please?"

Buddha, how I long to take my mother into my arms one last time. But I don't want to keep her from her happiness. I have caused her more than enough pain, hunger, suffering, and heartache. No matter how much I want to hug her, I can't hurt my beloved Ma again. I can't...I couldn't. I just couldn't do it!

Moy sat on her heels, rocking back and forth and raising her hands skyward, as she begged in Chinese and Khmer, for heaven to give her mother back to her. But Buddha had no mercy upon the poor girl. Suddenly, Moy jumped to her feet, grabbed her grandpa's spirit stand, and threw it down. Then she searched feverishly through every bag for all the pictures of her Grandpa and tore them to shreds, crying and screaming all the time. Finally, Pon's wife and daughter took some of the pictures away from her. They pulled her away from the mess she had made of the spirit stand—the rice can, broken bowls, and chopsticks were scattered all over the place.

28

Moy returned to sit next to her mother. Then she jumped to her feet and went to the red bag to get Keem's jewelry. Crying and holding it close to her chest, she sat down again next to her mother. Three days earlier, Keem had told her where to find the jewelry.

Keem warned Moy, "If something happen to me, don't tell anyone about the gold. Go live with Pon's family. They look like nice people. You must dress me in the pale-pink suit I buy for New Year, three year ago. You must bury me next to Grandpa's grave."

When Pon's wife saw Moy holding the small bag, she and her daughter asked to see what it was and tried to take it away from her. Moy struggled at first but finally gave in. When Pon's wife opened the bag, everyone screamed, "She have so much gold!" As Moy sat there crying for her mother, she watched the three walls of the house being torn down from the outside. The *vultures* took everything they could lay their hands on and ran off with it. Moy didn't care if they took the gold or clothes to exchange for food—all she wanted was to have her mother back.

Not wanting to hold her mother for fear of making her unhappy, Moy began to shake all over again. "Ma!" she cried. "Who look after me now? I not know anyone. Ma, I not want to live without you! Take me with you, Ma!" Moy screamed and cried until she couldn't scream and cry anymore. She could see the front of her house was packed with people; some women were crying along with her, tears running from their eyes. She stretched her hands out to her mother, hopping up and down on her backside and knees as if she could make her mother come back to life again. She was crying, "Ma, come back, come back to me. I be good child to you. You not have to worry. When I grow up, I take care of you. I not have anyone to love me, Ma, if you not come back. I not have anyone to love me, just you, Ma. Come back! Come back, Ma!" Still crying, Moy looked at her beloved mother's face. Keem's eyes were open, as if she wanted to look at her beloved daughter. Her mouth was open, as if she wanted to speak to her daughter again, but couldn't.

Keem's eyes were open. Now she saw what she had done to her only child. She had protected her child the best she knew how. She had loved her child like no other mother could. But now she was leaving her only child alone, in a world with no one to love her and care for her as she had. She saw now. She had given up too soon and gone to the happy world, leaving her child in a hateful land with unkind people. She had seen her little girl would live alone and unloved as she had and would suffer the same torture as she. Although her little girl would not be seeing her anymore, Keem kept her eyes open and watched over her little girl like a good spirit, keeping her daughter from harm as best as she could.

Keem's mouth was open, as if she wanted to tell her little girl how sorry she was for leaving her. Keem's mouth was open. Keem saw. She had chosen the wrong people to care for her daughter. Keem's mouth was open. She could talk to her only child whenever she wanted and tell Moy what step to take and where to go for safety. And her daughter would hear her. Not with her ears, but with her heart. Spirit or no spirit, she, Keem Lai, was still a good, caring, understanding, and loving mother. For as long as her little girl walked upon Mother Earth and beneath Father Sky, she would protect her child, always.

29

There were three suitcases left for Moy. Still crying, she went thought them and found Keem's favorite pink suit. Pon's wife and daughter had already washed her mother with a wet towel and combed her hair. Moy asked them to help her undress her mother and put the new clothes on her. They said to put the new ones over the old, because Keem was too stiff. Moy couldn't do what she wanted without their help, so she gave in tearfully.

Someone had put a can of uncooked rice and three burning pieces of incense about five inches from Keem's head. There were two lit candles beside her spirit stand. Moy took two handfuls of five-hundred ning bills and tucked them into her mother's hands, which were folded on her chest.

As if she hadn't been through enough trouble and pain, in came one of the Khmer Rouge. He wasn't carrying a gun. But he was the headman of the town. He stopped by the wall-less house and shouted at Moy, "Stop yell and cry like someone die!"

When he saw Keem's body laid out in front of Moy, he still shouted at her to stop crying. "Dead not come back to life with your scream and cry. I can't sleep with you scream like this! Now stop cry!" he shouted at the grief-stricken child, who had just lost her mother. It was like he was not human and had no feeling for anyone or anything but his sleep. When she didn't stop, he shouted angrily, "If you not stop cry, I send buddy brother over and shoot you away!" Then he turned toward the townspeople and shouted at them, "You never see dead person before? Go back to work! You want to die one by one like this family? Go to work!"

Pon asked if he could take a section of the wooden wall to carry the body away. Looking with hatred into Moy's tearful face, the Khmer Rouge replied, "Human dead and dead not need anything, living do."

Pon was mad. He and his wife didn't give up, and finally the Khmer Rouge told them, "Take three board and no more."

Several women dragged Moy from the bed and took her to Pon's house. They left her there. She sat crying for a long time and suddenly began feeling afraid of her dead mother. Then it was like someone was telling her she had to go back and see her mother again. She got up and walked back to the house, still crying. When she got there, she found her mother lying on the boards in front of the wall-less house. She had no blanket or small towel to cover her. Her eyes and mouth were still open. Then a strange thing happened.

Moy was afraid of her dead mother. She couldn't stop! She wanted to, but she couldn't stop walking! She couldn't stop to look at her mother's body. She walked past the house and her mother's body quickly, not knowing where she was going. Then she turned around and walked by again, glancing at her mother's body from the corner of her eye. She returned to Pon's house, no longer crying. It was as if her mother's spirit wanted her to see her beautiful body one more time before burial, like Keem's spirit was trying to tell her something as she passed not once, but twice, without crying but feeling afraid.

Once she got back to Pon's house, she started crying again. The witch doctor, Pon's wife, and their daughter had gotten there before her. Pon's daughter told Moy that when she and her mother had opened Keem's suitcases, it was like a force of blackness came over their faces so powerful that they couldn't see anything. They hadn't wanted to take anything, Pon's wife told Moy. They just wanted to see what was in there. But Keem's spirit was mean and powerful. Keem's spirit didn't want anyone to touch what belonged to her daughter.

The witch doctor didn't say anything about the opening of Keem's suitcases. However, he had a bucket of water in front of Pon's house. He dipped his fingers in the water and ran them around in the bucket, whispering softly. Then he had Moy stand in front of him. He had a small metal bowl in his hand, which he dipped into the bucket for the water. Then he poured the water in the metal bowl over Moy's head and kept on whispering. His free hand rubbed around Moy's head gently. The witch doctor told Moy to rub her face, arms, hands, body, legs, and feet, while he poured the holy water over her head. After the witch doctor had bathed her with the holy water, he had small red strands of thread, like a choker and bracelet, in his hands. He kept on whispering, blowing on the chocker and bracelet. Then he had the holy red choker and bracelet around Moy's neck and right wrist. He whispered some more and blew around

Moy's neck and wrist. The witch doctor told Moy the holy red choker and bracelet would keep her spirit from leaving her body and protect her from harmful
ghosts and spirits.

Moy stood in front of the witch doctor, not caring what he did to her. She
never said a word. Her heart had died with her beloved mother, and she didn't
want to live anymore. That night, Moy slept with Pon's wife. Outside, rain
poured down in a wall of water. The angry sky was filling with irritating light-
ning and thunder, and the wind was howling so furiously that it made Mother
Earth tremble under Moy's new bed. Thunder boomed so loud that no one could
hear his or her own thoughts. Moy had never thought the black night could pity
anyone, but that night, it did. It screamed as hard and cried as many tears as
Moy had over her dead mother. It screamed and cried for Moy too, because she
was all alone now. And it screamed and cried for her broken heart. But most of
all, it screamed and cried for the injustice, bloodshed, pain, suffering, threats of
murder, and betrayal the little girl would still have to live through, with no one
to help but herself.

The next day, through her tears and isolation, Moy heard the townspeople
say that the rain was her mother's tears. The loud sound of thunder was her
mother's screaming voice, showing her anger and broken heart for leaving her
daughter. They said if they were not careful with Moy, Keem would take the
girl's spirit with her; or if anyone harmed her daughter in any way, Keem would
take revenge upon them. It seemed the whole town, except Moy, was afraid of
Keem's spirit.

30

On the third day after Keem's death, Moy was sitting in front of Pon's house eating a piece of boiled corn. Then she found herself getting up and walking toward the small stream, crying as she followed the narrow footpath. She came to the small stream, crossed it, and continued to the right into the thick jungle, calling for her mother.

"Ma, where are you? I want you," she kept whispering as tears rolled from her eyes. Not knowing where she was going, she kept walking and found herself at Grandpa's grave. Looking at it with hate in her young eyes, she walked past it, while whispering in Chinese for her mother. She walked round and around, losing track of time. Then she felt something cold and slimy beneath her feet. Looking down, she saw she was standing on top of a mound of dead leaves and branches. There was a horrible smell coming from it that she would remember for the rest of her life. She didn't stop to investigate it then. Later on, she realized she had stepped on a dead body.

Moy kept on walking around some more. Then as if someone was telling her something, she turned around and walked past Grandpa's grave again, without looking at it. Not far from Grandpa's grave, suddenly, Moy fell to her hands and knees, like someone was pulling her down! For the first time, she screamed aloud, "Ma! Ma! Where are you? Ma, where are you?" She sobbed softy, like she needed her mother to comfort her after her fall. When neither Keem nor anyone else came, she sat there crying until her whole body shook. Then she saw something in front of her.

A few inches from her hands was a small hole, perfectly circular. Directly behind the hole was a mound of freshly dug earth with two large pine branches on top. Right next to the mound were the three boards. It was her mother Keem Lai's grave. The men hadn't even bothered to use the boards under the body as a burial platform. And the boards were covered with small red ants. Keem Lai didn't even have a small towel to cover her beautiful face, and her beautiful back was placed onto the Mother Earth's chest. Mother Earth got to wrap her loving arms around Keem Lai's bare face, hands, arms, body, and feet. Mother Earth got to love Keem Lai that much more than all the others under her care.

Moy broke down and cried harder. She recognized and remembered those three boards. She remembered when she had walked past the house and seen her mother's body lying on those three boards in front of the house, three days earlier. She stayed there, kneeling, hands on her lap, crying for a long time. Then it was like someone told her to get up, and she obeyed like a good little girl. She stood up slowly and looked down at the grave, wiping tears away with the back of her hands. All of a sudden, she felt scared! It was like someone was telling her to turn around and walk away from the grave, without a backward glance. Moy wanted to look back. But it was like someone was telling her, "Don't look back and never come back again!" Moy was very scared without knowing why, and she walked through the forest like someone was guiding her way *out*.

Once she was out of the thick forest, she began to feel more frightened without knowing why. She hadn't been afraid in the forest, even when she stepped on that slimy thing. But now, she felt more frightened than she had ever felt before—even the time in Siem Reap when she was five and she saw the soldiers covered with blood and the dead being carried from the streets. Back then, her mother had been there to comfort her, but now she had only herself.

When Moy got to the small stream, she stopped, remembering one time she and her mother had come there to fish. They didn't get any fish, because they were too busy laughing and giggling over something. She remembered her mother came there often. Keem would walk into the water up to her waist and pull out the long water lily roots. She would take them home and boil them with a little salt for them to eat, so they could fill their empty stomachs.

Moy also remembered when she couldn't find her mother at home, she always came to the small stream looking for her there. When she got there, she would stop at the edge of the steam and call out to her mother, "Ma?" And Keem would turn and smile at her.

Now, looking at the small stream, Moy could see her mother smiling at her, just like she always did. Without thinking, Moy walked into water and waded up to where the water lily roots grew. Moy's hands reached out for them as her mother's had. Then she heard someone calling her name.

She turned to look and saw the silver sun had turned orange and was on its way to its new kingdom. A bird was flying toward it. *Ma is free now—free from all the injustice her own mother did to her, free from what the Cambodian people did to her, free from all the suffering, pain, and tears. She is more beautiful than the orange sun and freer than that bird.*

She had the beauty of the Five Colors of the Most Powerful and the freedom of the freest eagle on Mother Earth and under Father Sky. All her life, she had had to live with little love and much injustice and hatred. Now she was in a world of justice, love, and happiness. Now she had as much power as the Queen of the Air and the Queen of Justice and Love. And she was following the father she had trusted and loved all her life into their new kingdom. *Lady Keem Lai* had finally found love and power and was at peace, at the age of forty-two.

Epilogue

The face of that sad girl is sort of fading away, and I see myself in the mirror again. *You see? I do know you, don't I?* I continue to look at the woman in the mirror. *You may be free one day, but not yet,* I say from my heart to the woman looking back at me, *There may be a way for you to be free. But first…*

Outside the mirror, I smile softly, and the woman in there smiles back. I turn slowly away from her and walk out the door.

THE END OF BOOK ONE

Heaven Is Calling for You

Goodbye is an awkward Word,

You knew Heaven was
Calling for you
But say nothing.

Love sparkled in
Your eyes as
You stared upon
My face and
Secretly,

You taking the
Memories,
Of my appearance
To your
New kingdom with you.

You had shed many
Teardrops and laughter
And left your
Foot patches from the
Mountainsides all
The way up to the
Mountaintops,

Gather leaves
For cooking
Fire in Chain,
For your beloved
Grandma,
Then left her
Behind,

Goodbye is an awkward.

You came over sea
And gave birth to
Me.
Your during was
To love me.

Now I'm 13
And you're leaving me.
The years was short, but
Memories will live and last.

You had fulfilled
Your during, and
Your new kingdom
Is waiting for you.

Your new assignment
is now due, and
You must return to
Heaven.
Mine Ma Keem Lai,
And
**Mine Grandpa
Wong Lai**.

Yours,

Moy
Luong Ung-Lai

3/21/2012

127

I don't know how old my mother was when each of these pictures was taken. She told me she took them in China. The picture of Ma with the bike was taken in Cambodia.

Ma told me, "I take this picture, when you five month old and still inside my belly!"

This picture was taken in Cambodia.

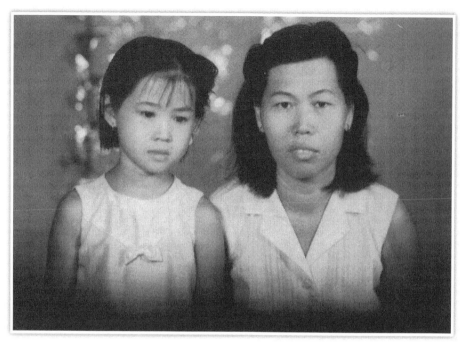

This is the only picture I have of my mother and me together. We took this picture in Phnom Penh, during Chinese New Year.

March 14, 2012

Author's Note

Life is full of mysteries. I started the *The Freedom...Cage* on February 27, 1987. It took me over thirty years to understand and realize the scenes between the witch doctor and the voice that came from my mother's lips, which are described in chapter 25. The witch doctor didn't make the deal with voice to save my mother; he was making the deal to save me. Pon's wife knew my mother was going to die, and my mother also knew. My grandpa didn't come after my mother. He wanted me. If he got me, he'd get Ma. My mother would not have lived a day longer if I had died. After Grandpa's death, and then to lose me? No way—she wouldn't have survived. But my mother made sure the deal was sealed. She'd go and leave me to be left alone and unharmed. I had a painful, painful stomachache. I could have died from that. But my mother said, "Whatever happen, let me receive them all. But let my child good, good."

I didn't understand it then. But as I was retyping the book into the computer and editing it at the same time, it hit me. Why would the witch doctor make a deal with the voice to save my mother when everyone, even I, knew Ma was going to die? Why wouldn't he know? Since I left Cambodia and for first time in over thirty years, I felt like someone was telling me to reread *The Freedom...Cage* and then retype it. Ma's and Grandpa's spirits and some powerful spirits high above in heaven wanted me to know the truth. I could be wrong; it's your call.

I did try getting *The Freedom...Cage* published a few times, but each time I thought about it, I always felt heavyhearted and like something was missing. But I didn't know what. I ended the books the way I wanted. Now, I know the answer. And I'll share it with you. I went to high school to learn the alphabet when I was eighteen years old. Six years after I escaped from Cambodia, I wrote *The Freedom...Cage*. Spelling and grammar were my weaknesses and still are.

I cleaned people's houses and got paid three dollars per hour. I worked in the supermarket, the five-and-dime store, and a clothing store in Boston while in school and saved every penny. When I finished the manuscript, I had the spelling and grammar cleaned up, and I didn't read it for over twenty-one years. Recently, all of a sudden, I wanted to get the book published! I told the publisher I had a book. I was ready to send it out after the publisher told me what to do. Then... it was like someone told me, "Read it first." The book was about 110 pages long (in font size 12), and some pages ended up with only two short sentences. I read only fifty pages...My mother and grandpa always said, "If it is good, then say it. If it is not good, don't say it," or "Say just one or two words, people will hear you."

Well, I'm not as nice or as forgiving as my mother or grandpa. But I'll make it brief. If you, my readers, paid me by the hour over a couple thousand dollars to clean up your manuscript, and then you found out there are misspellings, like "understood" spelled with three O's, and underlining in black ink, how would you feel?

That explained why I always felt so heavyhearted and like something was missing whenever I wanted to get *The Freedom...Cage* published. My mother's and grandpa's spirits were not happy their story was being treated as a moneymaker and without any respect for them. I think my mother's and grandpa's spirits wanted me to wait until I could read and understand properly and correct all the mistakes. I retyped, did some rewriting, and edited the whole book anew. As I did, my mother's and grandpa's powerful spirits guided me and showed me how to right the wrongs. I retyped, rewrote, and reedited the whole book, and I understand more things in the stories. I cried as hard as I did when I first wrote the book over twenty years ago. And I treasure my mother's and grandpa's love for me more than ever. (The poems and ninety-nine percent of "Before The Freedom...Cage" are new additions in the book.)

I don't know what you think of *The Freedom...Cage*. It was not how well or how much of the story I told that was important; it was when I had had enough, and I needed to rest, breathe, live, breathe, and relive again. *The Freedom...Cage II and Book III: Keem's Ring A Guiding Light* (the third book's subtitle) are combined into one. I started on them after I finished the first book. I can't say how long after I finished the first book.

At the time, I was in pain and all wrapped up in guilt. Sometimes, even nowadays, when I have a meal, in my mind, I'll see my grandpa on his hands and knees. I see that cooked baby mouse in his hands and how he ate it with a sweet, happy smile on his face. Other times, I see the picture of my mother after she drew her last breath—the look of injustice on her face, her open eyes and mouth, angry that she had to leave me at the mercy of the Khmer Rouge. I see that she didn't have a small towel to cover her beautiful face. Physically, I was fine; emotionally, I was beyond shattered.

As I am sitting here reediting this book, tears are still my best friend. It is like it was in 1987, when I was writing the *The Freedom...Cage*; for you, as the readers, *The Freedom...Cage* is just a story. But I tell you the truth, it was my *psychoanalyst*, the best psychoanalysis I could find. My psychoanalyst listens to my screams and blaming and sees my tears, anger, and guilt. But it never stops to listen or ask any questions, and above all, *The Freedom...Cage* never looks at my guilty face. My *psychoanalyst* lets me stop talking when I have had enough, and it never tells me when to come back.

My dear readers, I didn't tell you about my mother, grandfather, and my stories; my psychoanalyst, *The Freedom...Cage*, did. I thank you for your support by reading the *The Freedom...Cage*; I hope the publisher or publishers handle it with care and respect, and not as a moneymaker.

I don't know if *The Freedom...Cage* is going to make any money, but I know my mother's and grandpa's hearts were full of love. They always wanted to help the needy. They couldn't stand to see someone hungry. After what they had gone through, if they were here, I'm sure they would want me to have everything and share some with others. On behalf of my mother, Keem Lai, and my grandpa, Wong Lai, 10 percent of whatever *The Freedom...Cage* makes will go to a charity or charities. I can't name the charity until *The Freedom...Cage* has come to life.

* * *

I'll try to learn how to scan my manuscripts into my little notebook and turn them into words so that I can work on them. I'll get the *The Freedom...Cage II and III: Keem's Ring A Guiding Light* to you as soon as I can. Who wants to help me scan my manuscripts into my little notebook? I hate the computer when it won't work the way I want it to. I did try many times, but it won't scan my manuscripts in for me. I love the computer when it does what I want it to!

Well! After *The Freedom...Cage*, you and I need a break! How about a little laughter, adventure, romance, and magic? How does that sound? Good? Please, look for *Silver Moon, Tom Cupcake*, which will be coming soon. You and I need some fun. So relax! Kick back, but don't kick me! I'll bring you more laughter, more tears, and more romance! If you don't see *Silver Moon, Tom Cupcake* in your local bookstore, please ask them to look it up and order you a copy! Once again, thank you for your understanding and support...Thanks.

Your Author,
Luong

Made in the USA
Charleston, SC
03 July 2012